Wildly she thrust him away from her

Every muscle in him seemed to tense. "I should have guessed," he said harshly.

"Guessed what, Jason?"

"That desire is possible between us but not permissible."

"I don't understand."

"Don't you?" He swung around, fingers thrusting through his hair. "Because of Halloween night, I have to pay—and the price is high. Don't keep adding to it until I run out of revenue!"

She sat up, clutching her dress to her body. "What do you mean?"

"When you've grown up a little more, you may work out the answer." He walked past her, adding in a frozen voice, "Put on your dress or the staff might assume that we enjoy being married to each other."

As the door clo____ _____ tears creep___ _____

Books by Violet Winspear

HARLEQUIN PRESENTS

HARLEQUIN ROMANCES

These books may be available at your local bookseller.

For a list of all titles currently available,
send your name and address to:

Harlequin Reader Service
P.O. Box 52040, Phoenix, AZ 85072-2040
Canadian address: P.O. Box 2800, Postal Station A,
5170 Yonge St., Willowdale, Ont. M2N 5T5

VIOLET WINSPEAR

by love bewitched

Harlequin Books

TORONTO • NEW YORK • LONDON
AMSTERDAM • PARIS • SYDNEY • HAMBURG
STOCKHOLM • ATHENS • TOKYO • MILAN

Harlequin Presents first edition August 1984
ISBN 0-373-10718-8

Original hardcover edition published in 1984
by Mills & Boon Limited

CHAPTER ONE

THE china and glassware department at Grady's was at the rear of the store, and Dinah was arranging figurines on a display counter, her spectacles halfway down her nose as usual, when she saw a tall and familiar figure striding along one of the aisles in her direction.

She thought of ducking beneath the counter in an attempt to conceal herself, but Jason Devrel had the eyes of a hawk and there was no evading him. Dinah felt a rush of panic through her veins and she gave a gasp as a figurine slipped from her nerveless fingers and broke into pieces at her feet.

'Oh lord!'

'What have you done, Miss Stacey?' The supervisor hurried over to inspect the damage, while Dinah stared at Jason in the stone-grey suit that seemed to mould itself to his upright, graceful body.

'One of the Royal Doultons!' The supervisor gave Dinah an outraged look. 'You'll have to pay for it!'

Have to pay. The words echoed through Dinah's mind as Jason loomed over the counter and spoke in the authoritative voice that sent nervous chills up and down Dinah's spine.

'Will this cover the breakage?' He tossed several ten-pound notes on the counter.

'But it's the policy of the store,' said the supervisor, 'that if an employee breaks or damages an expensive item, then she has to pay for it out of her wages.'

'And no doubt go without lunch for a week.' Jason had a commanding air that matched his voice, and Dinah could see that the supervisor was impressed. 'Accidents will happen, so please accept the money.'

'Very well, sir.' The notes were counted and Dinah's nerves quivered in tune with the cash register. 'This gentleman wishes to be served, Miss Stacey, so don't stand there daydreaming.'

Dinah wasn't dreaming, she was still in shock from seeing Jason walk determinedly into her life again. There he stood, watching her intently as she nervously pushed her spectacles into place.

'Go away!' she wanted to cry across the counter at him. 'Leave me alone!'

That was all she had wanted when she had fled through the mist that always drifted along Devrel Drive early in the morning, rising up from the sea to cut the house off from the rest of Havenshore, so that it seemed to hang there on its crag as if its foundations weren't deep down in the granite of the cliffs.

Dinah had found herself on the station platform, her hair wet from the mist. She had boarded a train and several hours later had found herself in London, where at last she felt safely hidden away among the thousands of girls who worked in the various shops and offices.

Suddenly she was safe no more ... she was

threatened, and hurt again by the memories Jason brought with him.

'I know a young woman who collects tigers,' he said. 'May I see that fierce-looking creature that stands on the shelf behind you?'

Dinah fetched it without comment, and still she felt a weakness in her legs when she handed him the tiger, with its sleek shape and its cruelly beautiful face. As he handled it Jason watched her . . . relentless in the pursuit of his prey as any tiger.

'I'm sure she'll like this,' he said. 'Though it isn't quite as beautiful as the topaz one that stands on her bedside table, its eyes gleaming in the dark.'

'Why can't you leave me alone?' Dinah's face was chalk white so that her eyes blazed at him behind the rims of her spectacles. 'I want nothing more to do with you, Jason! I—I despise the very sight and sound of you—you know I do!'

'Naturally you're upset at seeing me, Dinah, but you started what I finished on Hallowe'en night, even if you won't admit it.' He spoke with a sureness which infuriated her so that, almost unaware, her hand closed upon a figurine as if to hurl it at him. She wanted to hurt him as she had been hurt . . . she wanted to see his assurance broken into pieces.

'I shouldn't do that,' he said. 'The store will run out of Royal Doulton ladies in crinoline dresses.'

'Go away before I call back the supervisor to say you're annoying me.' Dinah spoke through gritted teeth, 'You have no hold over me—I'm free of you now!'

'You'll never be free of me, Dinah. I've had a hold over you ever since you were a schoolgirl who came to my house to be my ward.'

'And what a peerless guardian you turned out to be! You're nothing but a smooth liar, Jason! Other people might mistake you for the essence of integrity, but I only know that you lied to me and left me to find out the real truth from other people. It hurt, Jason! Nothing in my life ever hurt so badly!'

His nostrils flared, a certain sign that his temper was on edge. 'You allowed a pair of gossiping women to upset you—I told you that, but you wouldn't listen to me.'

'I'd listened to other things you'd said and they all turned out to be false—false like those Hallowe'en masks we wore that night!'

Two months away from Jason had not eradicated a shadow of the scene which had taken place between them after the guests had gone home from the party. After the laughter had drifted away and the sound of the car engines, until there was only the sound of the sea splashing the cliffs.

'You can't make me stay here, not after this,' she had told him defiantly. 'You can't insist on it, not now I know the truth. I'm going away to make a life of my own. I'll be like other girls and work for my independence.'

When she had said that he had gripped her bruisingly by the shoulders, his face as if chiselled from stone. 'You came to me as a child,' he said. 'I looked after you and saw to it that no harm ever came to you—your life has been a sheltered one, here in my house. My house is your home and here you'll stay.'

'Never!' She couldn't face the thought of staying. There was nothing left to stay for . . . her tentative dreams had gone to dust and she felt crushed and belittled.

'I'm leaving, Jason. I'll find work in a—a department store. There's plenty of life going on in a store and I want to be part of it.'

'Don't talk nonsense!' Jason spoke the words bitingly. 'You talk as if you've been unhappy in my house, but you know that isn't true. Working in a store is for girls who need to earn their living, girls who have no resources. Do you really imagine in your innocence that being on your feet hour after hour is something to be envied? That waiting on demanding, irritable women is a pleasant way to spend your life? You're talking like a foolish girl in a soap opera!'

'You're bound to be sarcastic about it.' Dinah had felt herself getting the shakes, for it was always the same with Jason; always he insisted that he knew what was best for her.

'I want my independence, Jason, and I'm going to have it,' she defied him. 'For once in my life I'm going to do what *I* want, not what *you* want!'

He had stood there dark and grim, reminding her of what she had thought all those years ago when she first came into his house . . . that he was everything that was opposite to what she had adored in her father. A dark Lucifer, towering over her and making her heart pulsate inside her like a frightened bird.

He was some distant relation of her mother's, and when it was reported that her mother and father were not among the fortunate survivors from the air crash, Dinah had had to pack her few belongings and go in the big car to the big house on Devrel Drive to be the ward of Jason Devrel.

He was rich beyond anything Dinah had known with her parents, not that they had been poor. They'd been in show business and sometimes they flew to Hollywood or the Continent to appear in a film. They had been character actors rather than stars, and away at school Dinah had been shyly proud of confiding to the other girls that her parents were show people. She had tried not to mind when she was told that she didn't look anything like her glamorous mother.

One girl had suggested that she was a changeling, perhaps. While another had laughed and called her a cuckoo who had been dropped into a swallow's nest.

But whenever she looked into a mirror Dinah saw herself as owlish in her spectacles with the big round frames. When she came to live at Jason's house she secretly thought of the two of them as the owl and the tiger.

That was because of the graceful danger in the way he walked, and because it took such nerve to stand up to him. She had always felt little stabs of fear in his presence, from the very first day she came through the front door and he was standing in the hall, with the late afternoon sun striking down through the great windows, making him appear like a figure in the stained glass.

'You won't leave my house,' Jason said that night, but Dinah knew she would, because of what she had overheard during the course of the Hallowe'en party.

She had looked forward to the party and had found in an attic trunk a delightful peasant-girl costume which had belonged to Jason's grandmother. It was a Devrel tradition to throw three grand parties a year, one on Christmas Eve, another on the master's birthday, and the third on the night of Hallowe'en.

Dinah fully believed in the strangeness of Hallowe'en; for her it had its very own mystery, being the night when the witches and warlocks were supposed to be at their revels.

Dozens of people came to the house on Devrel Drive that night. A group of musicians were hired and there was dancing in the hall, beneath the glittering chandeliers that played over the couples in their fancy costumes and their masks. Only Jason chose not to wear costume, moving among his guests in one of his superb evening suits with a ruffled white shirt, his eyes gleaming through the slits of his black mask.

There was a feeling of additional excitement because tonight he had chosen to announce his engagement to Dinah. She had pleaded with him to let it be their secret for a while, but he had laughed at the notion of secrecy.

'Why shouldn't we tell everyone?' he asked. 'Most girls like the whole world to know that they're going to be married. Having second thoughts about becoming my wife?'

She shook her head, but doubts tingled inside her. 'Why me?' she asked him. Why, she wondered, when he hadn't said he loved her.

'Because I'm accustomed to your face,' he replied casually.

It was later, while Dinah was enjoying the cool air and a glass of champagne out on the terrace, that she overheard the conversation that tarnished the ring on her hand and quenched the glow inside her.

The two women were standing just inside the drawing-room where the windows stood open, and their voices drifted out past the long curtains. 'Of course,' said one of them, 'Jason's marrying the poor child because a young man of her own age isn't likely to fall in love with her. Just to think of it—all those years with a Devrel, and those two splendid schools he sent her to, and she's still such a gauche young thing.'

'Yes, to think of the best catch in the county becoming the husband of that Orphan Annie in glasses,' remarked the other woman, who had a sharper voice, which made the listening Dinah wince painfully. 'It's a wonder he hasn't arranged for her to have contact lenses; they'd make a difference.'

'Not everyone can tolerate them, Margaret, it's something to do with the tear ducts.'

'What a misalliance! I was quite taken aback when he made the announcement.'

'I daresay he feels responsible for her. He's taking this step because she's unlikely to attract anyone else, and it will scotch any rumour that they're living together as more than ward and guardian—if you get my meaning?'

There was a burst of suggestive laughter, then the voices drifted away, and for long moments Dinah stood there by the terrace wall and felt as if she couldn't take a deep breath. So the congratulations had been a mockery ... it had been evident to everyone that what Jason had proposed was a marriage of convenience.

It was after midnight when the guests began to depart, and in a while the house fell quiet except for the remote sound of the staff washing plates and cutlery in the pantry. Dinah wended her way up the wide panelled staircase and went to her suite in the Lady Grace wing, named after one of Jason's ancestors. It was said that the wing was haunted, but Dinah had never been disturbed by a flitting grey lady.

She closed her door quietly behind her and went to the big oak chest where she began to take articles of clothing out of the drawers. She folded them quickly and bundled them into a holdall. There were many nice things she would have to leave behind, cashmere sweaters and tailored jeans; long-skirted dresses and silk shirts along with riding outfits, tennis wear and sailing shorts, all from the best shops, including Harrods.

Jason had always insisted that she have nice outfits, though he must always have thought they were wasted on a girl as unattractive as herself.

She made a strangled sound in her throat and twisted his ring from her finger. What was she doing with a dazzling diamond on her hand? A girl everyone thought of as Orphan Annie in glasses!

She was zipping her bag when hard-boned knuckles rapped her bedroom door. At the sound Dinah's hand leapt nervously to her throat . . . in her haste to pack her belongings she had forgotten that Jason might come looking for her. She stared across the high-ceilinged room, an image of him engraved on her mind. Then the door handle turned and he stepped into her room.

He still wore his evening clothes and was smoking the remainder of a cigar. 'I expected you to come and have a quiet half hour with me in the——' He broke off as he noticed the half-closed holdall. 'What the devil are you doing, Dinah?'

'I—I'm leaving.'

'You're doing what?' A couple of strides brought him to the bedside, where he stood long and raking in the lamplight.

'I—I'm going away, Jason.' She unclosed her hand and his diamond ring glistened in her palm. 'Please take it back—I can't possibly marry you.'

'In the name of heaven——'

'I can't, Jason!' She took a quick, half-frightened step towards him and dropped the ring into a pocket of his jacket. Then she stepped quickly backwards, putting space between them. 'Y—you don't have to marry me in order to save me from being an old maid! Everyone at the party must have been having quite a laugh at my expense ... the gauche creature in the glasses whom you pitied ... who might if she went on living in your house cause people to wonder if our relationship was respectable!'

After that rush of words Dinah caught her breath. 'A man in your position, Jason, has to guard his reputation, even with someone plain like me——'

'What on earth has got into you?' His eyes glittered. 'What sort of rubbish are you talking?'

'I—I overheard some women talking about us—it was horrible, but it all made sense, and suddenly I realised that I couldn't stay here——'

'You're not going anywhere.' At the centres of his eyes a core of steel seemed to burn. 'Do you fondly imagine I'd allow that just because you heard a couple of women airing their tongues? Don't be so foolish! This is your home!'

'You can't keep me here—I'm going to call for a cab to come and pick me up——'

But even as she reached for the telephone Jason caught hold of her and gripped her with hands which could control with ease the most spirited horse in his stables. Always when Jason touched her Dinah was made aware of the controlled power in his six-foot body, and she felt it overwhelmingly right now.

'You're in a real state, aren't you?' Holding her firmly with one hand, he removed her spectacles and laid them aside, laying bare her blue myopic eyes so he could look into them. 'So the gossip of those women makes sense, does it? I'm marrying you so you won't be an old maid, and quenching the flames of scandal at the same time? How intriguing!'

'I felt as if pins were being pushed into me!' Dinah tried to shrug her shoulder out of his grip. 'Don't try and keep me here, Jason.'

'My dear child, what you'll do is unpack your bag, clean your teeth and hop into bed.'

'I'll go in the morning, and you can't stop me!'

'And where do you imagine you're going?'

'To find myself a job like other girls.' Dinah met his eyes and strove not to be afraid of his anger which could erupt with alarming force when he lost control of the temper that smouldered deep down in the dark Devrels ... more than once had their passions given birth to legends along this coastline.

Something flashed in his eyes as he looked down at Dinah, then his dark lashes cut across the look, concealing it. 'Tomorrow,' he said deliberately, 'I shall see about arranging a European tour. I think we'll start with France, then proceed to Venice, and I feel sure we'll have a good time.'

'Going around the museums?' She tossed back the hair from her eyes. 'I'd much rather work in a department store.'

'Where you'll come up against a few more women who like to be venomous with their forked tongues? In the city the people push and demand and strive to make a pound. They're used to it, but you aren't. There's no glamour to working in an office or a shop, so come to your senses, child—see reason!'

'You mean stay placable and be someone you can dominate.' Dinah took a steadying breath and instantly smelled the sea as it came in over the rocks of her guardian's private beach. 'Why don't you marry someone really suitable, Jason? Why choose your ward and give people the chance to call us a misalliance?'

'You're asking for a spanking!' He gave her a shake that flung her hair about. 'Unpack that holdall, put your garments back where they belong—and do it this instant!'

'You do it!' She glared up at him, white-faced, ready to spit and fight like a young cat. 'You put them away!'

Instead he caught the bag by the handle, tipped it and spilled garments all over the floor. 'Now put them away, and be quick about it,' he ordered.

A certain note had come into his voice that made Dinah clench her teeth. Mutinously she picked up an armful of her clothes, marched over to the oak chest and flung them into a drawer. She slammed it shut and caught sight of herself in the mirror . . . blue eyes alight with rebellion . . . and a tinge of fear, brought on by the darkness that surrounded the house, by the silence downstairs and her aloneness with Jason, looming there wide-shouldered, his lamplit shadow reaching to the ceiling.

'Do you mind going now I've done as I'm

told?' It was his dark shadow that she watched, waiting for him to move to the door ... praying for him to go.

'First I'll have your promise, Dinah, that you'll behave like an adult and forget this nonsense about running away.'

'I—I'm not making any promises.' Her voice shook and she could feel her heart thudding in her chest; she wouldn't surrender to his demands, not now she had found the courage to return his ring.

'I warn you,' he said, his eyes glittering as he caught and held her gaze, 'I'm not leaving until I have your word of honour that you won't run away; that you'll stay here, where you belong.'

'I don't belong to you, Jason. You haven't bought me just because you've paid for my education and fed and clothed me. Let me go out to work and I'll repay you out of my salary.'

'You obstinate child!' His shoulders, his entire body seemed to tauten, as if he was having to exert control over himself.

'Make your mind up, Jason, am I a child or an adult?' Her blue eyes fenced with his dark and steely ones. 'You seem confused by your attitude towards me, but the real truth is that you're a tyrant who wants his own way all the time, and you hate it because I've developed a mind of my own and want to follow my own inclinations instead of being another of your possessions in a house filled with them. Inanimate things on shelves that can't answer back, that can't complain when you move them about to suit your taste!'

Dinah tilted her chin and pushed a hand through her hair, feeling a nervous dampness at its roots; feeling the cling of her frilled petticoat against the small of her back. A few hours ago she had put on the peasant girl costume with a fairly light heart; now the petticoat, and the waistcoat, and the full sleeves of the dress felt burdensome and she wanted to be free of them.

'I'm tired of living in a house like a museum,' she flung at Jason. 'I won't be told any more what to wear, what to do, what to think. You're a tyrant!'

'You don't know what you're saying.' His lashes lay across the centres of his eyes and his look was dangerous. 'Tyrants treat people like dirt, and I've never treated you in that way. I've given you all the advantages, made sure that you went to the kind of schools where you'd meet intelligent, kindly girls from good families.'

'Yes, you've always picked my friends for me,' she agreed, 'and you didn't like it when I made friends with Cissie Lang. You said she was frivolous and a flirt, but I only care that Cissie likes to laugh. It isn't that she'll lead me astray, it's that you want to tie me down and keep me among your possessions. You talk about taking me to museums—lord, I've been living in one!'

'So my house is like a museum, is it?' Jason spoke the words in a low and threatening voice. 'Perhaps you think that I've no feelings to match?'

'That's exactly what I think, Jason.' A kind of recklessness had taken hold of her. 'You like to own things, and you'd like to put me in a glass case where you can pretend I'm not a normal human being who has to wash when she's dirty, eat when she's hungry, and cry when she's sad. You're the one who hasn't any normal feelings!'

'You insolent, ungrateful brat!' His nostrils flared and when he began to come towards her, she backed away, too quickly, so she stumbled over a footstool that sent her sprawling to the carpet. Jason straddled her, and then without any effort at all he swung her up into his powerful arms and carried her into the pool of lamplight that illumined the bed.

Suddenly he released her and she fell sprawling on to the satin bedspread. She crouched away from the look on Jason's face, for never before had she seen him so furious, not even when she had jumped Grasshopper at a fence and landed herself and the mare in a ditch of brackish mud where she had lain for almost two hours, trapped beneath the injured mare. The vet had had to put Grasshopper out of her misery, and Dinah had caught a chill which turned to pneumonia.

She felt almost as weak in this moment as she had felt when Jason carried her home that afternoon on his own mount Moonlight ... but he had held her gently, cradled so her muddy head was against his shoulder.

Here in her bedroom, on Hallowe'en night, he held her with hands like iron and even as she told herself that he would stop in a moment, when he had taught her enough of a lesson, Dinah knew that he'd lost control of his Devrel passions ...

those banked down fires that drew the attention of people even as they hesitated to approach him too closely.

That night Dinah learned to the utmost reaches of her being what it meant to be close to Jason . . . not as a guardian who protected her, but as a man who possessed her.

CHAPTER TWO

JASON left the shop, but what should have warned Dinah that he wasn't gone for good was the fact that he bought the porcelain tiger and had it gift wrapped.

She watched him walk out through the swing doors with a surge of relief. Perhaps she had convinced him that she despised the very sight of him and wanted never to see him again? As she got on with her work she clung to the hope that he had accepted her dismissal of him.

At last the working day was over. Grady's store ran a comfortable hostel that a number of the female staff were glad to use. Renting rooms had become quite expensive, and girls who lived on their own in the city were conscious of problems relating to the wave of crime that went hand in hand with the growing lack of employment to keep idle hands from pilfering and causing bodily harm to those who did have wages to take home.

Dinah hadn't liked the idea of renting a room and then having to turn it into a small fortress in order to keep someone from breaking in while she was at work . . . or when she was at home. She had chosen to live at the hostel, which was a few blocks from the store, and she liked to walk home at the end of the day, at least while the evenings were still light. She had been warned by the other girls that as winter approached and the days darkened it was wiser to share a cab or take a bus.

She had almost reached the hostel when she became aware that a car was trailing her. She was inclined to think at first that it was someone needing to ask for a direction, but when she glanced across the pavement and saw Jason seated behind the wheel of the Jaguar she felt her heart jolt. When the car stopped just a few yards ahead of her Dinah was tempted to turn and run ... but in that instant he flung open the door and in a couple of strides had reached her.

'Come with me,' he said. 'We have to talk.'

'We have nothing to say to each other ...' Dinah backed away, then flushed painfully as the action recalled that night at the house. She could almost feel herself falling again as Jason caught her by the arm, and somehow she didn't protest when he drew her to his car and shut her inside.

He drove to the Knightsbridge hotel where he was staying and took her into the cocktail lounge where the lights were dim and shielding. He ordered a couple of brandies and they sat at a table in a far corner of the lounge, away from the people at the bar.

'You need that.' He placed her brandy closer to her hand, clenched on the rim of the table. 'Don't refuse to drink it.'

'How did you manage to find me?' She raised the glass and put it to her lips.

He studied her a moment before replying. 'By a process of elimination, Dinah. You had told me that you wanted to work in a department store, so

I've been checking up on them. It occurred to me that you might use a different name from your own, and when my enquiries at Grady's revealed that a Miss Stacey was a fairly new employee there, I remembered that your mother's stage name was Sylvia Stacey. It's a form of fraud, you know, to give your employers a false name—you could get into trouble.'

Dinah flinched and swallowed a mouthful of brandy. 'Are you the man who's going to get me—into trouble?' She turned her gaze away from him and watched other couples smiling at each other; one pair were holding hands across their table, uncaring if they were observed.

'You're very pale, Dinah.' Jason cut through the silence between them. 'Drink some more of your brandy.'

'I—I didn't want you to come looking for me,' Dinah said tensely. 'Why couldn't you stay away? Why couldn't you leave me alone?'

'When you were nine, Dinah, you became my responsibility, and you'll always be so.'

'That's nonsense!' She gripped the glass that held her brandy as if she needed something solid to cling to. 'I'm over twenty now—I'm a woman!'

'You're a headstrong girl,' he corrected her, and there was a strange note in his voice which she couldn't quite place . . . Jason had never been a tender man, and she had discovered that he could be a ruthless one. Her eyes flicked his face, but it was a mask of distinction which told her nothing.

'I'll stay and have this drink with you,' she

said, 'and then I'm going. I have my own life to lead and you—you have no place in it.'

From across the table he watched her inscrutably; nature had arranged his features so he had a brooding, imperious look, black brows beneath thick hair the shading of dark armour. As always he was impeccably turned out in a light-grey flannel suit and a grey shirt with white collar and cuffs.

'Do you seriously expect me to believe that you enjoy working in that store, where you take orders from that rather grim-faced woman whom I presume is your supervisor?' The depth and deliberation of his voice matched his looks.

Dinah gave him a remote smile. 'I'd rather have her for my supervisor than you, Jason.'

'Really?' The only sign that her remark angered him was the tightening of the muscles in his hard jawline.

'I've grown used to the work and I quite like it,' she asserted. 'I've learned at last to stand on my own two feet.'

'When I entered the store this morning you looked ready to topple over,' he drawled.

'I—I was surprised to see you.' Dinah could feel each nerve in her body beating out the rhythm of her heart. 'I didn't realise that you'd bother to track me down, not after you'd got what you wanted from me.'

She heard him catch his breath and wildly hoped that she'd jabbed through his armour to his heart . . . if he had one that was penetrable?

'If you don't know by now, Dinah, that you're

part of my life, then you never will know it.' He spoke sombrely. 'You became part of it from the first day you came to my house on Devrel Drive, a bit of a child in a school frock and a pudding of a hat, gazing at me there in the hall with big sad eyes.'

'And you were remembering that about me on Hallowe'en night, Jason?' Suddenly Dinah was enjoying being cruel, though she remained sceptical about hurting a man who seemed so invulnerable.

'Sometimes, Dinah, a stronger hand than our own pushes us over the edge of reason, and you were driving me hard that night.' His gaze was upon her face but his eyes were remote, as if he was reviewing those scenes they had shared, culminating on the bed with the twist-wood posts. Long gone were the scratches from his face, but not the memories stored in his mind. Dinah felt a mortifying wave of heat sweep over her, leaving burning residues in those parts of her that were so vulnerably female.

'If you've come searching for me so you can say you're sorry, then forget it!' Her voice struck cold through the wave of heat.

'I've searched you out so we can be married,' he said, his voice deep but toneless. 'I still consider that we're engaged.'

'Married?' Scorn registered in her eyes. 'You— you can't seriously believe that I'll marry *you*? Hasn't it sunk in yet, Jason, that I despise you? Won't your arrogance let you believe such a thing?'

'I want to make amends to you.' Again he spoke quietly, and without emotion, almost as if he were proposing a business merger relating to the bank.

'What you really mean, Jason, is that you want me back in your house on Devrel Drive so you can run my life again. You talk of making amends, but that isn't your style at all, Jason. You were born into a family which has always given orders, and your father dying when you were just a kid made it certain that you'd grow up in charge of everything.'

'We both lost our parents when we were young,' he reminded her.

'My father wasn't the same as yours, born to be a banker with money and power in his hands. My father was kind and good and funny and he adored my mother. Do you imagine I haven't heard the story of your mother's unhappy life with a man much older than she, who had no patience with her youthful follies? Wasn't that why she turned her face to the wall and stopped fighting to live when you were born? I've seen her gravestone . . . she was only twenty-two when she died.'

'You're being rather cruel, Dinah, reminding me of my mother's wasted life.' Jason didn't raise his voice, but the flame-tips of anger were showing in his eyes.

'If I've learned how to say bitter things, then blame yourself,' she replied.

'Perhaps I do, but cruelty doesn't become you, child. You haven't the tone of voice for it, nor the look in the eyes.' His eyes flicked over her face, with shaded depressions beneath her cheekbones, a slight nose that made her spectacles seem too large, and a wide mouth with a full lower lip that would have been called sensuous had it belonged to a self-confident blonde. But Dinah's hair just missed being blonde, and her eyes could never decide whether to be blue or grey.

Suddenly Jason leaned across the table and held her eyes in a long look. 'You don't look well, Dinah—are you working too hard, or not eating regularly? Are you—all right?'

'Of course I am.' She braced herself against that searching look he was giving her . . . as if he sensed a secret.

'There's something about you—you must tell me what's wrong!' A note of urgency had come into his voice. 'You owe me that!'

'I owe you nothing, Jason. You owe me nothing. The slate is clean.' She managed to sound surprisingly composed.

'The slate can never be wiped clean,' he argued, 'not while we still have on our minds what happened between us the night of the Hallowe'en party. I wasn't proud of myself and when I found that you had gone, that you had actually run off, I was at my wits' end to know what to do. I searched everywhere but you had vanished out of sight. I tried, child, to forget that night but it haunted my days. I even told myself that it was something inevitable between us.'

'Inevitable?' she echoed. 'How can you say that? I never gave you any reason to—to behave

as you did. Y-you didn't have to punish me in
that way.'

'Punish you?' His defined features seemed to
twist for a moment. 'Is that how you think of it?'

'Of course I've been punished.' Suddenly there
were tears in her eyes, brimming through her
lashes. She looked away from him, a sob
strangled in her throat. Her profile was sad and
pale. 'Let me be, Jason. Let's part now, before
we say or do anything more to each other.'

'We're not parting, Dinah, not now I've found
you.' There was an obdurate set to his jaw.
'You're coming home with me and I'm not taking
a refusal. You're going to take up where you left
off, being part of my establishment.'

'You can't be serious?' She brushed a teardrop
from her cheek, ashamed of herself for being
weak in front of him when she had to be strong;
when she had to show him that she was
independent at last. 'Wild horses wouldn't drag
me back into your house!'

He caught his breath, almost as if he felt a jab
of pain. 'I'm not saying it will be easy for you,
Dinah, but it's where you belong, even if you
persist in denying it.'

'What exactly do you mean, Jason?' She
wanted to hurt his pride and humble him, make
him feel something of her own mortification. 'Are
you implying that we're going to take up where
we left off the night of the party? Is that what you
have in mind?'

He sat back against the wall of the leathered
banquette and his lashes lay heavy across his

eyes, which brooded upon her face for silent moments. The cocktail lounge had become more crowded and the sounds of conversation washed along the shores of Dinah's isolation with this man she had prayed never to see again. She didn't quite know what she felt when she looked at him. He was the one person in the world whom she knew intimately ... he was the close and distant stranger.

'I have to make you forget that night,' he said heavily.

'I'll forget if you go out of my life and leave me alone!'

'Leave you alone in the city with all its violence?'

'Violence?' she murmured, and swept a look from his wide shoulders to his strong hands, reminding him without words of his own behaviour.

His black brows drew together, then his eyes raked her face and slid down over her figure. 'Dinah,' he spoke her name with the utmost gravity, 'have I given you a child?'

The shock of the words seemed to slide in like a blade under her ribs; she was on the point of leaping to her feet so that she might run from him when he caught her by the hand, almost crushing the fine bones.

'Stay,' he said.

She couldn't have done otherwise, for suddenly she felt as if she had no strength left to fight him. Her legs wouldn't have supported her out of the cocktail lounge; she would have fallen down in a heap and made a spectacle of herself. She sat there dumbly, her head slightly bowed. Jason still held her hand and his gaze was insistent.

'You have to tell me, Dinah. I have to know—I have the right to know!'

'Y-you have no rights.' She shook her head defiantly.

'If you're carrying my child, then I've every sort of right. Tell me—one way or the other!'

'Really,' she forced a laugh, 'you don't have to worry about me, not in this day and age. We don't live in Victorian times—no woman needs to have a child she doesn't want, and I've already made my arrangements——'

'I can't believe I'm hearing you,' he broke in. 'My God, you're talking about killing the child, aren't you? Do you think I'd let you do such a thing?'

'You have no choice.' She spoke coldly because talking about the matter made her feel cold, afraid, and cheap.

'My foolish girl, it has everything to do with me.' Jason drew her cold hand deep within his, where the warmth and strength should have made her feel better. Instead when she looked into his face she wanted to hurl bitter words at him; she wanted to accuse him and remind him that he had despoiled her and she would never forgive him . . . never.

'Dinah,' he said, almost gently for him, 'hasn't it occurred to you that if you hadn't run away from me, we'd be man and wife by now?'

She answered his words with a scornful look.

'You'll say anything, Jason, in order to get your own way. You can't bear not to have things your way! It's all part of your arrogance and now—now you want me to believe that you want to marry me. Do you honestly suppose that I'll say yes and meekly submit to giving myself to you for always? You must be out of your mind!'

'There are times, Dinah, when we're all a little mad, times when we don't quite understand ourselves, but one thing is very certain, I've found you in time and can stop you from doing something you'd always regret—something that would scar your mind and leave you ashamed.'

'Doesn't it shame you?' she asked, 'that you've placed me in this predicament?'

'Very much,' he admitted, 'but things will seem better when we're married, and I'm going to arrange it right away.'

'No, Jason.' She shook her head and kept her chin firmly tilted. 'I'm not giving in that easily, just so your conscience can be eased and we can both wear a mask of respectability and pretend that we suit each other. The real truth is that without realising it I was being trained to become your pliable and undemanding consort. There was little danger that some dashing young man would come along and sweep me off my feet. If I harboured such hopes, you dismissed them, for love seems to have played no part in your scheme. I wonder, Jason, if you've felt a spark of love in your life.'

He sat silent, his eyes brooding behind his lashes. 'I've cared for you, haven't I?' he said finally.

'People care that their cats should eat their chopped liver,' Dinah rejoined. 'People care that their roofs shouldn't leak and let in the rain. Love is something different—an emotion you'll never stoop to feeling because it might make you vulnerable and less prone to wanting to crack the whip.'

'So that's your opinion of me.' He spoke sardonically, but his eyes resting upon her face held a shade of concern, for beneath her cheekbones the shadows thinned her face so it looked hurt.

'Who knows, Jason,' she didn't want him studying her so intently, 'I might have met someone who likes me. What would be your reaction if I had?'

He frowned. 'I don't quite know, Dinah.'

'You haven't given it a thought, Jason, because like everyone else you think I haven't the allure that attracts a young man.'

'If every woman had to be alluring, then very few would be wives,' he rejoined. 'Tell me, why do you care so much that a pair of gossiping women called you Orphan Annie in glasses?'

'Because it made me realise how little our engagement meant.'

'I don't get your point, Dinah.'

'A man like you, Jason, with a mania for filling your house with genuine works of art. Everyone expected you to produce a fiancée to match your collection, and instead you chose me . . . the owl among the Monet lilies and the Dégas dancers!'

'Stop it, Dinah!' He leaned forward tensely.

'You're hurting both of us, don't you realise that?'

'I'm hurting you?' She made herself laugh. 'That makes a change, I must say!'

'If I've hurt you, Dinah——' Jason spread his lean hands as if at a loss for the words that might convince her that he was repentant. 'Anyway, you're going to marry me and to the devil with other people and their opinions. What do they matter? The important thing is that I've found you, when I feared——'

'Fear?' she broke in, running her eyes over his face and taking in the firm strength of his shoulders. 'What have you to fear, Jason, that it might leak out that you made your ward pregnant?'

'Dinah, we must stop this!'

'You forced this child on me!'

'Dinah!'

'Humiliating words, aren't they, Jason? Always you've forced your wants and your ways on to me—*you*, always you!'

'For your own good, for the most part.'

'This?' She pressed a hand against herself. 'This is for my own good? You—you're so presumptuous! You don't seem to have taken it in that a dozen gold rings on my hand can't give me back my self-respect and my right to give myself to a man I might love. You took away the fact that I was a person in my own right and I—I hate you for that. I have no respect for you, Jason, and I never shall have!'

'All the same, you're having my child, and it's

a child I happen to want.' He spoke the words in a low and forceful voice. 'I want you to have the baby, Dinah, and nothing on this earth will make me stand by while you destroy a life we made together—in whatever circumstances. I'll tie your hands. I'll lock you up. I'll make a prisoner of you rather than allow the slaughter of that baby!'

Dinah stared at him, for it was plain from the look on his face and from the way he spoke that he meant what he said. 'Jason, we live in the twentieth century. You can't shut me up in a tower and turn the key on me. The idea's ridiculous—crazy!'

'I daresay it is, but I'm prepared to do it.'

'So you can possess our child as you've possessed me?'

'I want the chance to love it, Dinah.'

'How touching!'

His jaw clenched. 'You may say what you like to me, Dinah, and you are welcome to hurt me, but I'll protect that child if it's the last thing I do.'

Dinah had seen him break in powerful thoroughbred horses, using raw strength as opposed to the whip and the ranting voice. One summer she had watched in horror while he had removed a ploughman's broken body from beneath the great wheels of a harvester. And more than once he had gone out with the lifeboat crew during a high storm when a trawler was in distress.

She knew all about his force of character . . . Hallowe'en night was shaded like a dark dream from which she felt she was still trying to awake.

'I lived in your house all that time,' she said quietly, 'but I never really knew the real you, did I?'

'Do any of us know other people?' he asked.

She shrugged tiredly. 'You'll dominate the child because that's your nature. You can't change.'

'My life, Dinah, was a rather lonely one. My parents were gone and I had neither brother nor sister. Then you came along, and though I like my house it has its shadows, and you—you with your bright mind—dispelled some of those shadows. When you were home from school, and then college, the house seemed less lonely, and I was grateful for that.'

'You have a strange way of showing your gratitude, Jason.'

'Is anyone perfect?' He said it almost harshly.

'Nothing's perfect any more.' She spoke with her head bowed. 'I won't marry you, thank you very much. I won't let you put that kind of shackle on me.'

'Very well, Dinah, I'll stop being polite.'

Something in his voice made her look up, and her heart gave a little kick as she saw in his eyes the Hallowe'en devils from which she had run into the mist that curled along Devrel Drive.

'Do they know at the store that you're having a baby?' he asked.

'Of course not!' Again Dinah's heart gave a throb. 'It's a standing job, so I'd be given notice to quit——'

She broke off, a dawning realisation in her eyes. 'You wouldn't tell them——?'

'Don't force me to, Dinah.'

'Oh, what a brute you are!' She shrank back in her seat, not a vestige of colour in her face. 'You'd actually do that to me?'

'According to you, Dinah, I've already done the ultimate to you.' His lips moved in a momentary smile. 'How can I sink any lower in your estimation? Yes, I'd approach the management of the store and inform them of your condition if there's no other way to make you see sense. By my count you need stay with me only seven months, then I'll set you free. You have my word on it.'

'Your word, Jason?' Her eyes watched him uncertainly. 'How could I trust you—I think I'd rather trust a rattlesnake not to bite me!'

'Thank you for the compliment, my dear, but I'm prepared to sign a legal document to the effect that when the child is handed over to me I'll start divorce proceedings. If my lawyer draws up such an agreement then you can take me to court if I refuse to meet the demands in the document.'

He leaned back in his seat, but his eyes stayed intent upon her face. 'What do you say, Dinah? Throughout the next seven months you'll receive every care and attention, as I'd expect for a child of mine that you happen to be carrying. He or she will be a Devrel. The child will be my heir whether it's a girl or a boy. I doubt if I shall marry again, after you and I are divorced.'

Dinah listened to him in a kind of wonder. Could she actually believe the matter-of-fact things that he stated? Could she trust this man who had turned from being a guardian into a devil with dark and smouldering eyes on Hallowe'en night?

Even yet he seemed to exhibit very little guilt.

'I—don't know.' Her fingers twined about the stem of the glass which she had drained.

'Shall we have another brandy?' Jason beckoned the waiter who, despite being at the beck and call of half a dozen customers, came at once to their table and took Jason's order. Dinah had seen it happen a number of times. It wasn't only because he was a Devrel that he stood out in any crowd and commanded the attention. He had a natural authority, and only she had seen a side to him that was savage and passionate.

Looking at him now in his impeccable grey, every inch the gentleman, it was almost possible to believe that a devil had got into his heart and soul that night, when with those lean hands he had ripped off her peasant girl dress, torn the frilled petticoat without effort, and silenced her pleading with those lips that now proposed marriage.

'I have little faith in what you say,' Dinah told him candidly. 'I lived as your ward for eleven years, but still in many ways you're a stranger to me. Does anybody know you, Jason?'

'Do any of us really know ourselves?' he fenced. 'My lawyer is a discreet chap, and I do assure you that the agreement between us will be entirely legal and binding. I realise that I've made you hate me, so it should give you a certain satisfaction to marry me out of hate rather than love—wouldn't you agree?'

Their drinks came to the table and Jason raised his glass. 'I suggest that we drink to our forthcoming nuptials, my dear. We'll drink to the large sum of money I'll settle upon you the day you give birth to Jack or Carol Devrel.'

'So you've even thought of names,' she said, incredulously.

'Why not?' he asked. 'I often wished when I was a child that I had a brother named Jack, or a sister named Carol. They were names in a story book I had and I always liked them. As I'm to take sole charge of the child when it's born, then I'm entitled to choose the baby's name—won't you agree about that?'

Dinah picked up her own glass and watched Jason through quivering lashes. 'I always thought you—alarming,' she said. 'The day I entered your house you stood beneath the emblazoned windows in the hall, and you looked—frightening to me.'

He gave a shrug of the wide and powerful shoulders to which she had clung in shamed tears that Hallowe'en night. There had been a gloss of sweat on his brown skin and it had tasted of salt—his salt mingling with that of her tears.

'When will you go and see your lawyer?' she asked, a tang of brandy on her lips, helping to numb memory and bemuse her.

'Tomorrow if you like. He has his office here in the city—I'll telephone him tonight and make the appointment. You, in exchange, will ring and cancel your appointment.'

'At the clinic?' she murmured.

He inclined his head, his lips thinning until they were like flint.

'So once again you get your way, Jason.' She spoke resignedly, and couldn't deny the sense of relief that she felt inside her. It would have broken her heart to have had the baby murdered ... as she shuddered at the thought, Jason's fingers tightened on the brandy glass he held. All at once there was a shattering sound, and Dinah stared as brandy spilled over his fingers and ran down on the table. He dropped the broken pieces of glass and almost casually wrapped a white handkerchief about his bleeding hand.

'Jason!' she exclaimed.

'You wouldn't have thought that stone could bleed, would you?' He rose to his feet. 'Come, Dinah, I'll drive you to where you're living.'

'It isn't far—I can walk——'

'I'll drive you,' he said firmly.

CHAPTER THREE

ALMOST appropriately it was raining on the day that Dinah became the wife of Jason Devrel, beating down on the pavements, the rooftops of cars and the umbrellas that shielded people hurrying to offices and shops.

Dinah wore a simply styled suit and the colour matched her eyes. Jason wore charcoal-grey and as always his shirt looked crisp and very white against his skin ... Dinah couldn't help but admit to herself that he looked the epitome of distinction.

Upon the lapel of Dinah's suit gleamed the diamond and sapphire flower brooch which Jason had sent to her hotel suite. He had insisted that she move out of the hostel and for the past ten days, while arrangements for their marriage went ahead, she had been living in a quiet hotel just around the corner from where Jason was staying.

The marriage document had been drawn up and signed by Jason and herself; he had made her read every word in order to assure herself that she wasn't tied to him for life ... it set out quite plainly that she was permitted to seek a divorce from him as soon as it pleased her after the birth of their child. Her settlement was so staggering that she had protested, declaring that she didn't want his money and had every intention of working so she could keep herself and feel independent.

He had proved implacable. The money was being placed in a trust fund and she would never need to work unless that was her determined wish.

'We go our separate ways when the time comes,' he assured her. 'I shall never intrude upon you again.'

It wasn't until Jason slid the diamond band upon her finger that Dinah realised a very important factor ... they hadn't discussed the intimate side of their marriage ... whether they'd be sharing a bedroom or not.

She felt his dark gaze upon her as she made her responses to the vows, words about honour and being cherished until death parted them. Profound words, filled with meaning for couples whose hearts clamoured to be joined in holy wedlock.

Dinah's pulse beat quickly beneath the pressure of Jason's fingers and she wondered if he was thinking that the lovely old words had a significance which could never apply in their case.

After the ceremony they had champagne cocktails and delicious sandwiches in the company of a small group of friends whom Jason had invited to the wedding. The management of his hotel, where the reception was held, not only placed flowers around the room but provided them with an iced cake, which the guests insisted the bride and groom should cut together because it was supposed to bring good luck.

Jason laid his brown hand over Dinah's and the long blade of the knife slid through the white icing and the rich fruit cake, and everyone applauded. Most of the guests were content to believe that Dinah and Jason were a caring couple; they were totally unaware that Dinah was burdened by the true facts of her relationship to the man at her side, a champagne cocktail held in his hand, a smile quirking the edge of his lips as he responded to the traditional quips which a newly wed couple had to grin and bear.

Whatever Dinah's doubts, tinged as they were with bitterness, the reception was pleasant and the champagne helped her to relax and to give the appearance of a quietly happy bride. She looked beguiling in blue, and managed to laugh when someone asked why she had chosen not to be married in white.

'I'm one of your modern brides,' she smiled. 'I shall be able to wear this suit again and again, but a wedding dress is rather a white elephant once the big day is over.'

'All the same,' the woman protested, 'most young brides like a traditional white gown, and it isn't as if Jason has to count his pennies.'

'True.' Dinah assumed a casual look and tried not to notice that her waistline was being measured by the woman's eyes. Oh, let them all speculate . . . it seemed to be the done thing when a bride didn't wear white at her wedding. Let them wonder . . . they'd find out in due course that Jason had taken her to bed before the wedding ring was on her finger.

Something clutched at her heart, for how loveless that precipitate bridal had been!

At last they were leaving and their luggage was being stacked into the boot of their Jaguar. They were driving home to Havenshore, for Dinah had refused to even consider a honeymoon; her eyes cold and distant when Jason had suggested that they tour France or Italy. 'For my further education?' she had asked coldly. 'No, if I'm to spend the forseeable future bearing your offspring then I prefer to do so in surroundings that don't pretend to be romantic—such as Paris or Venice.'

'As you wish, Dinah.' He had made no attempt to try and persuade her, and she noticed his quizzical expression when he saw that someone had attached silver horseshoes and ribbons to the bumper of the car. They drove off in a hail of good wishes, then their guests dashed back into the hotel out of the rain. There was still some unopened champagne and they would carry on the party for a while longer, no doubt speculating on why the bridal pair chose to start their life together without the glamour of a honeymoon.

Dinah leaned back in her seat with a sigh. 'Thank goodness that's over! I never realised that getting married could be so nerve-racking.'

'Now you can relax,' said Jason. 'Everything went off smoothly, and you looked bridal without the white gown and the veiling.'

'Several of the women were curious,' Dinah murmured. 'I think they guessed that I wasn't what you'd call—pure any more.'

'Dinah!' he exclaimed. 'You're developing into a young cynic, and cynicism is incurable.'

'Wouldn't you have liked a bride all shining new and pure?'

'Stop dwelling on it,' he ordered. 'What does it matter what a few rather envious women think.'

'Envious, Jason? Why, because you've married me and made a Devrel of me?'

'I didn't mean that at all and you know it.' He drove along the Embankment where a veil of rain shimmered over the blending of buildings and the rigging of ships, adding rather than detracting from the very special beauty of the locality.

'Then what did you mean?' she persisted, the fingers of her right hand twisting the strange new ring on her left hand.

'They might envy your youthfulness and your bright mind . . . your vulnerability.'

Dinah wondered that he could even say that word when he had taken advantage himself of her vulnerability. She cast a quick look at his profile and it was as hard and defined as if cast in bronze. There was nothing vulnerable about Jason. He had the ability to put to his advantage even the mistakes which he made . . . including the fact that in marrying her, he acquired a Devrel heir without needing to be a faithful and loving husband until death parted them.

'Try and relax and stop using your mind as a motorway where questions keep flying back and forth,' he urged. 'Accept the fact that you are now a married lady.'

'Do you truly expect me to feel like a lady?'

'It takes more than one man to turn a woman into a tramp,' he said crisply. 'It isn't emblazoned across your forehead, little fool, that you're a brand new bride carrying a two-month baby— you look as slim as ever.'

'Don't pay me compliments, Jason. I don't want them from you.'

'You don't imagine I'll let you accept them from other men, do you?'

'Men don't make passes at girls in glasses,' she said flippantly. 'And I'm no more to you than an incubator on a pair of legs.'

'For the time it takes, Dinah, you are Mrs Jason Devrel, and I expect you to behave like a wife in front of other people even if you inwardly hate the sight of me.'

'You can be sure that I do, Jason.' She spoke quietly so the words could take effect ... a statement flung in anger was like a stone thrown at random, less likely to hit its mark.

'Be that as it may,' he rejoined, 'we've got to speak to each other like rational human beings.'

'You said in front of other people, Jason. Don't deprive me of the private pleasure of telling you that I no more regard you as a husband than I would a total stranger.'

'We aren't strangers, my dear Dinah. We never can be. We are linked by the child you carry.'

'Thanks to your devilry!'

'Dinah,' he gave a short laugh, 'are you never going to smile again? It always seemed to me that you inherited your father's sense of humour.'

'I can't quite bring myself to be humorous

these days. I'm carrying the can while you hide your real self behind an air of unruffled aloofness. I—I was looked at, back there at the wedding reception, as if you were doing me a favour—sorry I can't scintillate!' Her right hand covered her left one so she didn't have to be aware of the diamonds sparkling in the ring which to her mind was an expensive shackle . . . a constant reminder of how she came to be Jason's wife. 'If we've got to speak to each other, then let's be polite and leave it at that.'

'Like strangers sharing a table at a hotel?' he queried.

'If you like. I don't want to get involved in the kind of discussions that probably go on between a husband and wife.'

'That ceremony in church was real enough, Dinah. The man who held the book and tied the knot was a priest, so you're going to have to accept that for the next seven months we are husband and wife, and there are matters we have to discuss.'

'Why discuss anything, Jason, when you'll have your own way come hell or high water?'

'Did I insist on the regulation honeymoon?'

'No, because you were no more keen on it than I was.'

'That isn't quite true, Dinah.'

'You mean you're dying to be rowed along the Grand Canal in Venice in a gondola, serenaded by a gondolier in a straw hat?'

'Why not? It's what couples do on a honeymoon, or so I've heard.'

'No doubt they do lots of things that we shan't be doing,' she rejoined, hoping he got the point.

Jason gave a brief laugh, letting her know she had scored a hit without getting him in a vital spot. 'Y'know, I can't figure out if you're being childish or just plain churlish,' he drawled.

'Take your pick.'

'H'm, I have heard it said that if a woman isn't too joyous while she's carrying a child, then the poor little beggar is likely to have a sour outlook on life.'

'That's an old wives' tale.' She sat gazing through the windscreen at the wipers sweeping the raindrops back and forth across the screen . . . the blade was so ruthless and the drops of rain could do nothing but submit to their fate. She felt as if she had been swept off her feet and engulfed in a wave which had carried her into depths where unknown dangers still lurked. Her trust in Jason had been scattered to the four winds like those drops of water, and she sat here in unwanted intimacy with him, driving home to the house on Devrel Drive to be the mistress instead of the ward.

'I expect everyone at Havenshore will be titillated when you bring me home in such an interesting condition,' she remarked.

'Are you going to mind that there'll be a certain amount of gossip?' he wanted to know. 'It won't take them long to guess that we anticipated our wedding night.'

'Don't use that word,' she exclaimed. 'You know the real one!'

'I sometimes wonder.' He spoke almost to himself. 'There's no doubt that people are going to guess about the child, but it's our business, and I hardly believe that other residents of Havenshore are angels with spotless wings. We're all human and there are dark impulses in most of us.'

'It certainly can't be said of you, Jason, that you hide the fact that you're arrogantly aloof and darned sure of yourself!'

'I can't say that I'm sure of you, can I, Dinah?'

'You got what you wanted. I'm sitting here and I've got your ring on my finger.'

'What do you think of your ring?'

'As I'd expect, expensive.'

'I have another locked away in the safe at the house, and when we arrive home I'll present it to you. It belonged to my Spanish grandmother, so you can accept it as being from her. She was a rather lovely lady ... as you've seen from her portrait.'

Dinah had always admired the gold-framed portrait of Doña Manuela that hung in the drawing-room; it was from her that Jason had inherited much of his darkness, especially the thick lashes that shaded his dark eyes, and the proud bearing. She was aware that before she ever met him, he had often visited relatives in Andalucia where he had learned to go into the arena with the big bulls. The experience had honed his reflexes and given him a certain grace of movement which matadors acquired in the use of the cape.

It had also, Dinah felt sure, intensified in him the Latin attitude towards women. He had certainly proved it in her case! As a young girl growing up in his house she had been guarded and protected from the jostling, competitive world she had so longed to join when she finally left the exclusive environs of the college where her education was completed.

Her cry for freedom had aroused the savage in Jason, and he couldn't soothe her or quieten her fears, nor sweeten her bitterness by offering her the family heirlooms and speaking in that softened tone of his grandmother.

'I really do want you to have the ring; if you find the setting old-fashioned then the stones can be re-set.'

'It would hardly be worth it,' she replied in a cool voice. 'I shall only be wearing it for the next few months, until I'm free to leave you.'

'I want you to keep the ring, it will be yours for keeps.'

'I'll say one thing about you, Jason, you're quite a generous man—but you can afford to be, can't you?'

'Grudging praise, Dinah,' he shrugged.

'You're lucky to get any at all.' Her hands tightened together in her lap. 'There is one thing we should have discussed, and that's our sleeping arrangements. I—I refuse to share a bedroom with you, a-and you'd better not insist that I do.'

'My dear Dinah, I'm not such a boor that I expected you to let me share your bed. I know how little you want my company.'

'But I know you now, Jason—you're not above forcing me to do what you want. I—I wouldn't be with you right now if you hadn't forced your way into my bed!'

'You get real pleasure out of throwing that in my face, don't you, Dinah?'

'It's the only pleasure I am likely to get out of this—this marriage, so don't begrudge it me. You were telling me a short while ago that a woman should feel some joy while she's carrying, and I do enjoy reminding you that you're not the high and mighty gentleman that everyone takes you for!'

Jason made no reply but drove on in silence, and when Dinah stole a look at his face she saw that a nerve pulsed at the side of his mouth. Dinah wanted to feel a glow of satisfaction because she had got under his skin, but it had been a rather cheap jibe and it had left her biting her lip.

'I—I shouldn't have said that,' she said contritely.

'Don't apologise.' His voice held a distant note. 'You'll have to remind me again that I'm not a gentleman if I ever show signs of behaving as I did on Hallowe'en night—maybe a devil got into me, who knows?'

After that he just drove and didn't speak, and Dinah settled down in her seat, leaning her head back against the soft leather and closing her eyes. Tiredness had crept over her; an emotional tiredness rather than a physical one. She hadn't worked at the department store since Jason found her, so she wasn't bodily worn out by those long hours upon her feet.

The store and its customers, some of them quite as demanding as Jason had warned, and going home to the hostel to eat supper with the other girls who lived there, seemed very much in the past right now.

It had been something of an adventure and she didn't regret her attempt to be a working girl. It might have worked out had she not become pregnant with Jason's child ... how scared she had felt, and how alone, when she realised what had happened to her. She couldn't help but wonder if it had been relief rather than dismay which had overcome her when Jason had walked into Grady's store ten days ago.

His very tallness and sureness had made her feel that he would put things right and that she wouldn't have to endure the torment that many girls faced, that of having the embryo cut from her body.

She was back in Jason's keeping, safe within the confines of a marriage that would ensure the child's safety ... but would he keep his word and release her at the end of their seven months as man and wife? Even though it was all written out in a document, Dinah couldn't forget the adamant set of Jason's features when he had placed his signature alongside hers.

She knew in her heart that she'd never trust him again, but there was a strength and sureness about him that made her feel less alone and tormented by those doubts which had kept her restless night after night at the hostel.

There had seemed only one terrible solution to her problem . . . arranging to be rid of the child seemed the only way out for a girl who worked as a salesgirl and lived in a hostel . . . how could she have the baby only to see it taken away for adoption? But by marrying Jason, loveless as the union was, she had at least ensured that the child would be reared by its natural father and there was no question that his son or daughter would receive every advantage, as she herself had done during those years as his ward.

All at once tears were scalding her eyes and there was such an ache in her throat that she could hardly bear it. That ache spread inexorably through her body . . . she was married to a man of substance and her child would never want for a thing, yet Dinah felt a terrible sense of loss rather than gain.

'Are you feeling cold?' Jason asked suddenly. 'Shall I turn on the heater?'

'No—I'm all right.' She struggled to control her tears, but a couple wended their way down her face and slicked her lips with their saltiness . . . she prayed that Jason wouldn't glance at her and notice her tears, which she didn't dare to wipe away. She had wept *that night* and had vowed afterwards that she wouldn't ever let him break her pride again.

'You gave a shiver that I actually felt.' A note of concern threaded his voice. 'I noticed that you didn't eat much at the reception and you're probably feeling hungry. We'll stop in a while and have a meal.'

'All right,' she said, then added: 'You do it well, don't you, Jason?'

'Do what, Dinah?'

'The concerned husband act.'

'I don't happen to be acting.'

'Oh—having guilt feelings, Jason?'

'A few.'

'Only a few?' she said dryly.

'As many as will satisfy you. It would seem that it's the only kind of satisfaction you want from me.'

'What are you hinting?' Dinah felt herself go tense. 'If you're getting the idea that I want you for a real husband then you'd better start thinking again. That's the last thing I want! I couldn't bear you to touch me!'

'Don't get worked up, child. You'll do yourself some sort of damage if you keep getting all tensed up—you must learn how to relax.'

'You're to blame if I'm worked up,' she retorted. 'I—I mistrust you so—you say one thing, but your eyes say something else.'

'Whatever do you mean by that remark, Dinah?' He shot her a look, for though he had turned off the motorway the country road ahead of them was rather narrow, with unexpected turns, and he had to watch for oncoming vehicles. 'You do have the oddest fancies, but I suppose they're part of your condition.'

'You—you seem to delight in my condition!' Dinah's eyes flashed with sudden temper, banishing her weepy feeling. 'It's a pity you're not the one who's going to have to waddle about looking like a two-legged barrel!'

He gave a laugh. 'That's better, Dinah. Now you look spirited rather than dispirited, and your sense of humour is coming back.'

'I wasn't being funny,' she snapped. 'If men had to have the babies, they wouldn't be so keen on—on doing what makes them!'

'Appalling grammar, child, but I get the message. But are you convinced that it's only men who enjoy making—love?'

'Love?' She gritted her teeth. 'Is that what it's called?'

'Sex, then, if you prefer the term.'

'I prefer nothing connected with sex—especially your sort!'

He heaved a sigh, only slightly exaggerated. 'I'm not to be forgiven, then?'

'Jason, don't try to get round me with your dubious charm. Don't forget what you said when you proposed marriage—you said it was hate not love that bound us together. It's what most women feel for the man who does to them what you did to me—do you want me to say the word?'

'If you need to say it, Dinah.'

The word was written across her mind, but her voice wouldn't project it. She turned her gaze away from Jason and laid her face against the cool leather of her seat. She didn't want to look at him in the well-cut suit which made him look distinguished . . . she wanted to remember the way he had lain beside her as the first threads of daylight crept into her room, his skin like cinnamon against the white sheets, his black hair in disarray, his spent passion allowing her to creep from his side, to find shirt and jeans and her handbag. Then she had run from his house as if pursued by devils.

While she remembered what he was truly like beneath that look of culture and breeding she wouldn't fall into the trap of believing that his protectiveness was genuine.

What he had done to her that night was to betray her trust in him after all those years she had been his ward. Today at their wedding his friends had obviously thought of him as the epitome of aloof but genuine charm, and to all outward appearance he did have an air about him. It was in the way he held his head high, in the way he carried his shoulders, even that enigmatic smile that sometimes touched his mouth indicated a man of reserve and good taste.

A man faintly amused by other people who had affairs or allowed themselves to be led into debt. People who drank too much and made themselves look foolish.

Dinah wondered if she was the only person in the world who had ever seen Jason lose control of himself.

In a little while she drifted off to sleep . . . then came awake with a start, believing she had only closed her eyes for a short while. Instead the rain had died away and the westering sun was reflected in the windows of a rambling house. She sat up, pushing the hair out of her eyes.

'Why didn't you wake me?'

'I decided to let you sleep on.' Jason sat there with an elbow on the wheel, watching her in the silence of the car which now stood in the driveway which had seemed so endless that morning she had run away from the Devrel mansion high on the cliffs of Havenshore.

When they stepped from the car a wind rustled in the leaves of the big trees that lined the drive; the rain had freshened the air and Dinah took several deep breaths in order to bring herself more widely awake.

As they made their way up the steps to the huge front door, she felt a tightening of her nerves as Jason slid an arm about her waist. When they stepped in under the arch of the porch Jason turned to her.

'In the next seven months we're going to need all the luck we can muster, so how about allowing me to lift you over the threshold?'

'No——' she stood there stiff-spined and unreceptive, 'I don't think it's a good idea.'

'We have to be friends at the very least.' And the next moment, with that easy yet alarming strength of his, he lifted her clear off her feet and directly the door was opened by his butler, Jason carried Dinah into the hall, into the light spilling down from big lamps attached to the great span of oaken beams.

Dinah stared into her husband's eyes. Jason was thirty-seven and he looked every one of those years. He had had to accept responsibilities quite early in his youth, and each lean cheek was clefted by a shadowed line and the blackness of his brows and lashes added depth to his eyes. His mouth alone revealed the opposing forces in his nature, for there was a boldness which the firm line of the upper lip controlled.

Above his eyes his hair swept back in raven thickness, his sideburns shading his jawline in almost a nineteenth-century style. It had often occurred to Dinah, while she had been growing up in his care, that he'd look at home in the clothing of that past century.

'Put me down, Jason.' She kept her voice steady, for his butler was watching them, eyes politely veiled.

'You weigh little more than when you were fifteen,' he said. 'Sometimes when you fell asleep in front of the television set I'd carry you up to your bed, remember?'

'Jason,' panic sharpened her voice, 'it's a pity you didn't always remember that I was your ward!'

'God!' He dropped her as if she had suddenly burned him; his eyes blazed down at her and she shrank away as if expecting a blow from his clenched fist.

She heard the drag of his breath. 'Today, Harding,' he said to his butler, 'Miss Dinah and I were married.'

'Indeed, sir?' Harding had a perfectly controlled voice. 'May I offer my congratulations?'

'If you feel you must, Harding.' Jason gave a brief and very cynical laugh. 'We hope for joy from marriage, don't we, but it's usually the sympathy that we need.'

Dinah stood there, her teeth almost breaking the skin of her fist clenched against her mouth. She had said a cruel thing to him, but surely he understood that there was no going back for either of them to the days when she was an innocent girl in his house and he the guardian of that innocence?

He was the one who had destroyed it all ... with the help of two women talking spitefully behind the curtains of the drawing-room on the night when the witches brewed their mischief.

CHAPTER FOUR

So here she was, home again in the towered house on Devrel Drive, so long established on the Havenshore cliffs that the dreams and pains of all those past generations seemed to whisper in the night when the sea breezes rustled the ivy that cloaked the walls.

Coming home to the house she had fled from gave Dinah the strangest feeling, as if she stepped back behind invisible bars where she must wait out the next seven months as if it were a term of imprisonment.

That evening of their homecoming they dined on delicious soft-shelled crab and tangy white wine, followed by pears in vanilla with chocolate ice-cream. Jason had one of the best cooks available and he could well afford the Frenchman's salary. Like everything in his house the staff were hand-picked, and before dinner Dinah had been presented with a maid of her own, a young local girl named Hester, whose skin was flushed like a fresh apple and whose soft country tones soothed Dinah's abraded nerves.

'I'll take care of you fine, Miss Dinah,' the girl said. 'I know about your baby. Sir up and told me and said I was to see to it that you took proper care of yourself. He wants that baby real strong, you can see that.'

'Does he really?' Dinah spoke in a cool voice. 'It's easy for him to want it, he doesn't have to bring it into the world.'

'Having a baby doesn't have to hurt, Miss Dinah. You have to learn how to relax yourself and when the time comes the little mite will pop out like a nut from its shell, you mark me.'

Dinah couldn't suppress a smile, for the girl was no older than herself and yet she spoke like a young matron. 'How do you know it will be that easy?'

'I've got three sisters and four brothers,' Hester replied, 'and my ma sailed through all those births because she never gets flurried about anything. That's the secret, Miss Dinah, you take my word for it. Never let anything get you stirred up; just take things as they come, just like the fishes and the birds. You do that and you'll be fine.'

'Is that a promise?' asked Dinah, wishful that she could swim calmly along as the waves of an unwanted destiny swept over her. Nothing matched up to the romantic dreams she had sometimes indulged in at college ... vagrant longings and thoughts of love had been scattered like spindrift off the rocks far below the house of which she was now the mistress.

Watching Jason through a gust of his cigar smoke, Dinah wondered if giving birth to his child would be an easy experience, and she felt a twinge of resentment that becoming a father would be so easy for him.

They had withdrawn to his favourite room, the

music room, where his gleaming black grand
piano was companioned by a cabinet television
set and shelves of recordings and video tapes.
The furniture set around the room was in deep,
rich woods and was genuinely antique. Underfoot
were carpets in rich deep colours, laid over a
parquet floor that was never waxed beneath the
carpets for it took a high sheen that brought out
the tiger-like markings in the wood.

Dinah gazed around her and remembered those
evenings when Jason sat here at the grand piano
and played those beautiful nocturnes that drifted
out through the windows that opened on to a
terrace. There, deep in one of the cane chairs, she
would listen to the music and somewhere in the
garden a nightingale would echo the sound. Jason
had been taught the piano as a child, then had
neglected it for some years until suddenly in his
thirties he started to play again. He played well
. . . Jason did a lot of things with ease and facility.

As a teenager she had looked up to him, both
physically and mentally . . . perhaps sensing
unaware that they were heading for a clash of
wills.

This house on Devrel Drive had its history,
and was only about a mile from where a girl had
thrown herself from the high cliffs—the locals
said from love, possibly betrayed love.

Here in the music room there was a painting of
Jason's mother; a thing of vibrant beauty whose
flesh tones were almost alive on the canvas, the
eyes looking out from the pale and lovely face
filled with a kind of sadness, as if she already

knew that she wouldn't survive the birth of her son, whom she had been carrying when the portrait was executed. Her slim, ringed hands were folded in her lap, there against her body where Jason had lain inside her.

Was it being without a mother that had taught Jason to grow into such an aloof and confident man, as if he had deliberately armoured himself against sentimental feelings so they couldn't get inside him and cause him those wrenching bouts she sometimes had, so she wanted to cry out in order to relieve the anguish he had caused her.

'Has the wine gone to your legs?' Jason asked suddenly, watching her as she sank down on the carpet in front of the fire. He came and flicked ash among the flames, then locked the cigar back in his mouth as he gazed down at Dinah, towering over her darkly. 'Glad to be home?'

'The house does have its ambience,' she replied.

He regarded her through the smoke that twined about his face and lost itself in the darkness of his hair. Then he glanced across at the painting of his mother, studying it for several minutes before bringing his gaze back to Dinah. 'Your portrait should be added to that of my mother and grandmother, and all those other Devrel women hung here and there about the house. What do you say, Dinah?'

'Unlike those women,' she said deliberately, 'I shan't be staying long enough to be regarded as an established Devrel. I'd forget the idea, Jason.'

'We shall see.' With the toe of his shoe he

tapped a half-burned log into the centre of the fire. 'I like your dress, what colour do you call that?'

'Apricot.' The chiffon dress belonged to her days as his ward and she knew he had seen it on her before, but men rarely remembered a style, they more often remembered an impression created by a garment.

Memories moved at the back of Dinah's blue eyes and she knew that the dress belonged to her nineteenth birthday, when Jason had presented her with a string of pearls and clasped them about her neck. Even yet she could recall how the nape of her neck had tingled when his fingertips brushed the sensitive skin ... she had pulled away and for some reason her movement had caused the string of pearls to break. Jason had muttered an oath as the gleaming little globes had rained down on the floor, then hastily she had kneeled and collected them together in the palm of her hand.

That was why she had chosen to wear the apricot chiffon tonight, and through her lashes she watched him until she saw his mouth give a twist, telling her that the scene with the pearls had flashed back into his mind.

'Dammit!' he muttered, tossing the stub of his cigar into the fire. 'Pearls for bad luck, eh?'

'Did you say something, Jason?' she murmured.

'There's no doubt about it,' he said reflectively, 'a woman can be ruthless when she hates ... and sometimes when she loves.'

'The subject of love is taboo,' she rejoined, 'so shall we change the conversation?'

'Don't allow your feelings for me to fester away at your charm, Dinah.' Each word seemed to emerge as if he had chiselled them, hard and decisive as the look of his features. 'You have a charming simplicity, you know, and a lack of conceit ... rare combinations in a woman. I wouldn't want to see you lose those attributes.'

'Jason, aren't you talking like a man who locked the stable after the horse had vanished? You rate yourself a good horseman so you know very well that if you beat one down, it won't ever be proud again. It might sink its teeth into you, given the chance.'

'I'm merely holding out a little sugar.' His smile was brief and didn't reach his eyes. 'I'm certainly watching out for those sharp little teeth of yours. I've felt them!'

Instantly, as if he had pressed a release button, Dinah had an image of his bared brown shoulders indented by the marks of her teeth. He had laughed deep in his throat, almost as if he believed that she had bitten him in passion, wanting the taste of his skin as he thrust her over the edge of a brain-melting void where her cries sank low.

Dinah crouched on the carpet, staring at the iron dragons that stood sentinel in the great fireplace. Colour stained her cheeks, for it was so mortifying that he carried in his mind the same images of that Hallowe'en night ... she wanted to crawl away like a little dog on its stomach.

'Shall I switch on the television?' Jason asked, as if he also needed to banish those very personal images. 'There might be an old movie on one of the channels, or shall I show a video film? We've only watched *The Champ* about a dozen times; you know you love it.'

Dinah shook her head. They had watched the film together in happier times, and it involved that huggable little boy with the blond hair, and that scene at the end when the father died and the child kept crying out to him to open his eyes. The scene always broke her up, and if she started to cry tonight she doubted if she'd be able to stop.

Abruptly Jason sat down in one of the fireside chairs, and down there on the carpet Dinah found herself close to his long legs. His eyes looking down at her were piercing, like the sheen on very dark metal.

His gaze was impossible to evade, his eyes held her magnetised. 'Women like sitting on carpets like cats, but there's something of the cat in lots of women. They like to be bribed and petted.'

'What are you going to bribe me with——?' Her gaze slid to his nearest hand, then was dragged back again to his face. 'Don't you dare pet me!'

His mouth gave a slight twist as he took a small square box from the pocket of his black velvet smoking-jacket. He dropped it into her lap.

'Go on, open it,' he ordered.

'It's the ring you told me about, isn't it?'

'Yes.'

'I—I don't really want it, Jason.'

'I'm insisting.'

'In that case——' She shrugged and opened the box and the gems flashed in the band of deep gold; the setting was charmingly old-fashioned. It was the kind of ring that belonged on the hand of a beloved woman.

'Don't make me wear it,' she breathed.

'Why not?' Jason's voice came low from his throat.

'I'm sure your grandfather had it specially made for your grandmother.'

'The gems can be re-set, Dinah, if you prefer.'

'No, that would spoil the beauty of it.'

'Then if you find it beautiful, put it on.'

'I—it doesn't belong on my hand,' she protested.

'What makes you say that?'

'Y-you know——'

'Do I?'

She glanced up at him through a wing of her smooth hair; her eyes were shadowed. 'I think you should return it to the safe—save it for the woman who comes after me!'

'I told you, Dinah, I shan't marry again.'

'How can you be so sure?'

'I am sure. Now put the ring on, or shall I do it for you? I always intended you to have it.'

Reluctantly she pushed the ring up against her wedding band where the two sets of gems flashed and glowed together. When her term of being Jason's wife came to an end she would leave the rings behind . . . she wouldn't want any reminders of their marriage.

'I'm sure that didn't hurt,' Jason drawled, and abruptly he stood up and approached the Regency side-table where crystal and silver merged together. He poured measures of French brandy into a pair of crystal bowls on slender stems. He came back across the room and handed one of the stemmed bowls down to her. She cradled it in her hands and breathed the aroma of the cognac, and Jason did likewise, holding the crystal caressingly in his lean fingers. Dinah had always noticed that about him, the satisfaction that beautiful objects gave him.

This room in which they sat was beautiful, warm-toned from the clusters of wall lamps in brass brackets. Yards of thick ivory silk hung at the mullioned windows, beyond which the sea splashed the cliffs which held the foundations of the house.

'Well, this is almost like old times,' Jason remarked. 'You and I alone in this room, the two of us shut away from the world . . . when you were just a schoolgirl you used to say this house was like an enchanted sea castle, and you were never afraid when the winter fogs rolled in and isolated us.'

'You like being cut off from the rest of the world, don't you, Jason?' She looked up at him, young looking in her chiffon dress, her smooth hair reaching to her shoulders.

He smiled a little and tilted his brandy bowl, letting the golden cognac slide down his throat . . . almost a sensuous gesture. 'It isn't such a bad thing, Dinah, to shut the world out when we feel like it. It gives the mind and spirit a rest, for that world out there has become restless and tinged with the sulphur of erupting violence. I believe I'd have liked to have been born into the nineteenth century.'

'You would have looked well in the clothing the men wore then, and you have a turn-of-the-century attitude where women are concerned—you really do believe that women belong in the home, don't you, Jason? Kept in bondage to their lord and master!'

'Do you think of yourself as being in bondage to me, Dinah?'

'Yes,' she agreed. 'Our marriage couldn't mean anything else to me.'

He swirled his brandy silkily in the bowl. 'Are you keeping a notebook, my dear, filled with bitter little quips just for my benefit?'

'No, but it's a good idea. I shall have to get myself a notebook.'

As she finished speaking the rosewood clock on the mantelpiece began to chime, the silvery notes chiming through the room. 'Time,' Jason murmured, 'how much of it is needed to dilute certain memories. I feel like playing——'

Her hand jumped and brandy spilled on to her dress.

'The piano, my dear.' He stood up and went across to the piano and opened it, the ivory keys gleaming in the lamplight. 'Would you like to hear me play, Dinah?'

'I haven't anything better to do, Jason.' She dabbed at the skirt of her dress with her handkerchief and didn't look at him.

He drew out the piano stool and sat down, his hands running along the keyboard. Then he began very softly to play *Noche Triste*.

Sad at night, she thought, and then he spoke through the music. 'Did you know that this song has very romantic words?'

She shook her head, and he began to speak them in his deep voice, tinged always with a sardonic note. 'Beware of the wine of love. It must be savoured with love or it turns to tears. A lonely love can taste like a bitter wine. Beware when you taste it.'

'They don't sound like modern words,' she said.

'They weren't written in modern times.' He played on, drifting from one piece of music to another, and in a while Dinah felt herself drawn to the piano where she leaned in her youthful dress with the scooped neckline that revealed her fine skin and the fragile collarbones.

As the music faded, and as if suddenly she wanted to shatter the spell of it, she said in a brittle voice: 'I wonder how long it will be before I have to stop wearing my nice dresses?'

'I'll buy you others.' Jason closed the piano. 'Great smocks beneath which you can hide your horrid secret.'

'You're a swine, Jason!' She backed away from him. 'You enjoy it so much that you've got me imprisoned in this way!'

She walked away from him, and was terribly aware of his child within her body.

'My butterfly in chains.' He followed her

across the room, and in a sudden fury she swung round and struck at him, leaving the imprint of her fingers across his face.

'I want my time with you to go very quickly,' she panted. 'I want to be gone from your house!'

'We've only just arrived home.' He spoke very quietly and he showed no sign that she had hurt him, outwardly or inwardly.

'Oh, why did this have to happen?' She wrung her hands. 'I hate being like this—hate what you've turned me into!'

'Only a wife.'

'My feelings don't count, do they?' She glared at him. 'I believe you're proud of yourself!'

'I can't deny that I want you to have my baby.'

'Damn you to hell, Jason!'

'I'll agree that heaven's out of my reach,' he shrugged.

'You've a heart like quarry stone, do you know that?'

Looking ironic he touched his own breast. 'Feels normal.'

'This—this relationship of ours isn't normal!' She prowled about the room, picking up small objects of art that were placed here and there, fingering them, filled with the urge to break something he valued. The thing she most wanted to break was his heart . . . if only she knew how to do that!

'I—I've got an idea.' She faced him defiantly. 'Why don't you go travelling? Go to Europe and visit all those fascinating museums and art galleries—I'll be happy to stay here on my own, getting bigger and bigger. I'd prefer that. Why not go to Rome on your own—why do people go to Rome?'

'They go there to gaze at statues.'

'And what about Paris?'

'To see sculptured iron and civilised women.'

'What of London?'

'To see the lions in Trafalgar Square and ride on a red bus. Come with me, Dinah.'

She shook her head, her shoulders sagging. 'I'll soon be big as a red bus.'

'Nonsense, you're going to have a baby, not an elephant. You must try and look forward to the future.' Suddenly he was striding so forcibly towards her that she flung up a hand as if to ward him off.

'Don't—don't touch me!'

His eyes bored down into her and it was as if he struck the well of misery inside her, tears welled into her eyes and the hollows of her face were filled with hurt shadows.

'Dinah, my child, nothing is as bad as that.'

Angrily she wiped away the tears he had drawn from her—she had sworn she wouldn't cry again, but he made her want to howl and tear her hair. 'I—I'm biting on the berries of the bittersweet,' she said huskily. 'Don't you care?'

'They're sharp and poisonous, Dinah.'

'Our life together is poisoned!'

'Are you going to suffer like this all through our marriage?' he demanded.

'I expect so.'

'Then won't you let me comfort you a little?'

'I don't want your kind of comfort!' she said bitterly.

'Then have another brandy as a nightcap.'

'Why not?' She found her glass and handed it to him. 'Fill it to the brim and I'll go to bed drunk and forget everything!'

'My child——'

'I shall never be a child again—you've seen to that!'

Silence hung between them into which the scent of roses drifted, dark red roses clustered in a nearby bowl. There were many roses in the garden of the beast, she told herself.

Jason reached out a hand and stroked the hair from her brow, his touch lingering on its shining softness. 'You're so upset—tell me what I can do?'

'Afraid for your precious heir?' she asked. 'Afraid I shall lose it if I go on being so emotional?'

Then before he could reply she flung away his hand. 'Don't do that—I've told you that your touch makes me ill!'

With these words Dinah ran to the door and fumbled it open; she fled across the hall and ran up the stairs to the Lady Grace wing. There she came to a breathless halt, backing away from the door of her old bedroom as she remembered that she had been moved into a different suite of rooms . . . away from the bedroom which held a memory she could never run away from.

She hastened to her new bedroom, went inside and closed the door. The lock held a key and she turned it with a sharp click, then she went and lay on the bed, motionless but for the racing of her heart.

Jason wouldn't follow her, he wouldn't dare . . . not after she had said that awful thing to him. Gradually her heart quietened and she closed her eyes, letting the far down splashing of the sea upon the rocks soothe her nerves. Upon her outflung left hand she could feel the weight of Jason's rings . . . he had got his way and brought her home to his house, and here she must stay to have their loveless child.

CHAPTER FIVE

IN the following weeks two people came into Dinah's life whom she was to value. One of them was Rita Malcolm, a gynaecologist whom Jason had thoroughly checked before putting Dinah into her care.

Dr Malcolm was a woman of about forty, with dark hair worn in a nape knot and clever, compassionate eyes. She examined Dinah, took blood tests and went into all the usual details. Yes, Dinah could tell her exactly when the child had been conceived; it had been on Hallowe'en night.

'You're very certain,' the doctor smiled. 'A special night for you and your husband?'

Dinah sat there at the patient's side of the doctor's desk, her eyes shaded by her lashes. 'In a way,' she replied.

The doctor wrote down the date. 'Then we can expect the birth on or about the first of August. That's a nice summery month for a baby to be born, did you plan it that way?'

Dinah looked up startled. 'Oh—no!'

'I just wondered.' Rita Malcolm sat back in her desk chair and studied Dinah who looked very young and a trifle delicate in a cream mohair suit worn with tan-coloured chamois boots. The heart shape of her face was framed by pale gold hair, her lips looked soft and giving, but her blue eyes were reserved, veiled by the spectacles. They were the eyes of a girl lost in sad reflections rather than happy anticipation.

'You want this baby, don't you, Mrs Devrel?' The doctor eyed Dinah with a touch of concern. 'I know your husband is looking forward to the event, and though I've only recently met him I have the feeling that he'll make an excellent parent. The very fact that you have his support should make you feel secure about becoming a mother. Are you a little afraid? Some women are the first time, and it's only natural.'

'Have you any children?' Dinah had noticed the wide gold band on the doctor's left hand.

'Yes, I have twin sons away at university. My husband was a doctor, a very clever one, but he developed an incurable blood disease and I lost the only man I ever wanted to love.'

'I'm sorry.' Dinah wished she could confide the real source of her fears, that it made all the difference having a baby if the parents loved each other.

'Well, Mrs Devrel, I can inform you that you're a healthy young woman but rather high-strung at the present time and not eating as well as you should. I want you to put on a little weight.'

'But I'll look huge!' Dinah protested.

Dr Malcolm smiled. 'I doubt it. You're rather too thin at the present and it takes a certain amount of strength to carry a child with comfort. This is your first child and we don't want any problems if they can be avoided.'

'Are there likely to be problems?' A frightened look came into Dinah's eyes.

'None that I can see at the present time, just so long as you obey orders and eat well and try to steady those nerves of yours. Have you always been a rather nervy type of girl?'

'Now and again,' Dinah admitted. She had always been inclined to restlessness while Jason could sit still for an hour, legs outstretched, smoking one of his slim cigars. She had tried to smoke one and had nearly choked. 'You must be made of leather inside and out,' she had told him.

'You shouldn't be so jumpy,' the doctor said. 'You've no money worries, not with a husband who owns most of Havenshore and that wonderful house high on the cliffs. Can I make a guess? I realise that you're not long married, so obviously you've been lovers—oh, don't get me wrong! I'm not laying down the law about that.'

Dinah's hands clenched together in her lap, her fingernails almost breaking the skin of her palms.

'What is it—aren't you in love with your husband, Mrs Devrel?'

'He—he was my guardian.' The admission seemed to emerge of its own accord from Dinah's tremulous lips.

'I see.' The doctor tapped the rubbered end of a pencil on the papers in front of her. 'So it led to—marriage. Well, as I see it, you're a fortunate young woman. He's quite an aristocrat, isn't he, and a scion of one of the oldest families in the West Country. Is it true what I've heard about him, that he has Spanish blood in his veins?'

'Yes, his grandmother was the daughter of a Spanish *conde*.'

'Then I'll say it again,' a smile shaped the doctor's mouth, 'you're a fortunate girl to have such a man for a husband. He's attractive enough to be a full-blooded Spaniard.'

'Do you think so?' Dinah spoke with a hardened note in her voice.

'You must surely think so yourself, Mrs Devrel. I've driven past your house on Devrel Drive and it looks such a fascinating place. Perhaps one of these evenings you'll be kind enough to invite me to dinner?'

'You'd be welcome,' Dinah said truthfully.

'Good. Now don't forget what I've said about improving your appetite, and in the meantime I'll arrange for you to attend relaxation classes. They're held in this building and take place two afternoons a week. They're fun, and you'll get to meet other young women who are facing childbirth for the first time. I'm sure their company will help dilute your apprehension.'

They said goodbye and Dinah walked out to the car, the sleek Mercedes-Benz driven by Jenkins, the chauffeur who was courting her maid Hester.

Jason refused to let her drive the sports car which he had given her when she left college, which she had left behind in the garage when she had fled away from him that misty morning last November the first. She hadn't wanted anything more of him, but now he had her back in his keeping he refused to return the car keys to her.

He said he didn't trust her to drive it efficiently in her present state of mind, and he didn't want his child smashed up in an accident.

His child, she thought, as she climbed into the comfort of the Mercedes. *Always his damned child!*

'Is everything all right, Mrs Devrel?' Jenkins was eyeing her with concern. 'The doctor hasn't given you upsetting news about the young one, has she, ma'am?'

'You don't have to worry, Jenkins, the precious Devrel heir is in perfect order.' Dinah couldn't keep a tart note out of her voice, for it now seemed that everyone knew about her condition and, naturally, they were more concerned for the Devrel child than they were for its reluctant mother.

The chauffeur broke into a smile. 'Hester told me you're set on a son, ma'am.'

'I am!' she asserted. 'Boys are tougher than girls and don't get so put upon.'

'I suppose you could say so, ma'am, but girls are prettier.' Jenkins carefully closed the door of the car—as if Dinah was made of china in which tea was served in the afternoons—and looking smart in his buff-coloured uniform he climbed behind the wheel and drove her home through a countryside, where a sudden snowstorm in the night had left the fields and hedges and farmhouses looking like a Christmas card.

For the first time in eleven years Dinah hadn't spent Christmas in Jason's house, where a splendid party always took place, with a towering tree in the hall decorated with glittering baubles and presents for everyone who worked for Jason.

This year she had worked overtime at the store, caught up in the excitement of the crowds that came in droves to spend their money on family and friends. Later on she had gone out carol singing with some of the girls and for a while her worries had been held at bay. On Christmas morning she had attended service at a local church, and pausing in the porchway to look at the Nativity she had felt an alarming clutch of guilt ... had known, perhaps, that she would never be able to bring herself to be rid of the child which in his angry passion Jason had sired.

Now here she was, safely tucked into a car rug, reassured by a doctor that all was well, and on her way home to a delicious lunch. It was true that she wasn't eating well, but that was because she wasn't happy.

Dinah sometimes felt that she'd never be happy again ... never know what it felt like to be lighthearted.

That evening, just before she and Jason went in to dinner, he informed her that Dr Malcolm had telephoned and told him that she was in good shape apart from her nerves, and that she must eat well and keep up her strength and vitality.

Dinah shrugged, still slender enough to get into an opal silk dress with supple, almost gothic lines, the neck cowled, with a silver chain about the waist.

She swirled in front of Jason like a model. 'Perhaps I want to keep my figure for as long as possible,' she mocked. 'I'm not just a container for your precious child, I am a person in my own right, but all I keep hearing is that I must do what's best for the valuable bundle I'm carrying around. Now I've got to stuff myself so I'll be even more enormous! All very well for you, Jason!'

'Stop being such a little grumbler!' He came over to her and, before she could step away, placed his hands on her hipbones, pulling her against him and forcibly holding her rebellious blue gaze.

'It's about time someone told you that being an expectant mother is making you appealing, and as I am your husband that right is mine. Your skin is like silk; it's finer than the fabric of this dress, and there's just a dash of wild colour in your cheeks. I know you don't want me to pay you compliments, Dinah. I know you hate them coming from me. You believe they're a prelude to my visiting your bedroom and having my devilish way with you, isn't that so?'

The colour deepened under her skin. Then recalling that Dr Malcolm had called him attractive, she ran her gaze over his face, seeing the Latin thrust of his cheekbones and shadows of perhaps a Moorish heritage in his dark eyes. Summer or winter his skin was the colour of burnt cinnamon, so that his always brief smile showed teeth white and strong.

'Do you ever want me?' she asked him boldly.

'Of course.' He said it without blinking an eyelash; said it looking her shamelessly in the face. 'I wouldn't be normal if I didn't want you—you are my wife, aren't you?'

Dinah took this calmly enough, but inwardly she felt as if wings fluttered, wildly enough to make her want to gasp. 'Haven't you a mistress?' she asked. 'You can well afford one, and I understand that men in your position usually have a lady tucked away in rooms somewhere. Someone admiring and sympathetic who makes up for a wife who's uninterested in sex.'

When she said this, Jason's grip tightened on her hipbones and a steely glitter came into his eyes. 'You deserve a spanking, do you know that? You think you can provoke me and that I'll do nothing about it because of your condition. I'm warning you not to try me too hard . . . my control might snap and there wouldn't be any way to stop me from having my way . . . you know that, don't you?'

Yes, she remembered how uncontrolled he could be, and her heart gave a frightened leap. She despised herself for letting him frighten her, but he was so much bigger than she, so powerful with that span of shoulder bone, hard muscle strapping his chest and the thighs she could feel through the silk of her dress.

Then quite out of the blue she heard herself saying to him: 'What would you do, Jason, if I said you could come to my room and make—love to me?'

'I'd come,' he rejoined.

'But I'm never going to invite you, Jason, you realise that?'

'Yes, I realise it, Dinah.'

'I never dreamed that my so-called guardian was really a brute!'

'That's a nice expression to use, my dear.' He spoke quietly, but seething in his eyes was a look that warned her that she was trespassing upon his pride.

'How would you describe yourself?' she asked. 'How would you describe what took place between us—don't tell me you have a romantic term for it?'

'There are some things between a man and a woman that can't be explained in exact terms,' he replied. 'The wearing of civilised clothing, of eating at table with a knife and fork, and washing the dirt off one's skin, these aren't always a sign that we've emerged fully from the caves. We make clever conversation and we put men on the moon, but underneath it all we're still the servants of our impulses.'

'You might be,' Dinah rejoined. 'Isn't it a fact that the Moors ruled Andalucia and left not only fountains in Spanish gardens but the desert in Spanish veins?'

'Yes, it's a fact.' Jason released her and turned away, his eyes hooded. 'Such strains will be in that baby you are carrying; does it upset you, my dear?'

'Why should it? You're the one who's going to rear him.'

Jason swung to face her. 'So you've decided that we're having a son?'

Dinah fingered her waist chain. 'Men like to

have a son, don't they? You have a great deal to hand on—this house, your land, the bank and its branches. You've said you won't marry again.'

'Nor will I, Dinah.' His gaze was straight as a blade, unwavering when he added: 'One taste of marriage will be sufficient for me, and if the child does turn out to be a boy, then he'll grow up as I did, his mother an unknown quantity ... a portrait on a wall.'

It was during dinner that Jason told Dinah that a celebrated artist was coming to Havenshore in order to paint her portrait. 'His name is Barry Sothern. He's particularly good at painting women and has work on exhibition at some of the best galleries.'

'But why should you want a portrait of me?' Dinah pushed the prongs of her fork into a wedge of perfectly cooked steak. 'I should think you'd be glad to forget me instead of having me hung on a wall to remind you of our dismal marriage.'

'I'm thinking of the child,' Jason replied, raising to his lips his glass of Montrachet. 'He or she will want to know something of the mother who left the father, wouldn't you say?'

'I—I'm not sure.' Dinah twisted the stem of her wine glass in her fingers, for suddenly her appetite was fickle again and she didn't fancy any more dinner. 'Your mother died, so you had nothing to reproach her for ... I shall leave voluntarily, if I survive the birth and don't end up like your mother.'

'That isn't going to happen to you.' He spoke with abrupt curtness. 'Aren't you going to finish your dinner? Leon was told to prepare one of your favourite dishes, and now you sit there letting the food grow cold.'

'Oh, do stop it, Jason!' She pushed her plate away from her. 'Stop fussing over my appetite and tell me some more about this artist—is he young or old?'

'He's about forty. I once saw a lovely thing of his in the Tate Gallery, a portrait of girl on a stretch of wild beach, her bare feet in the surf, the wind tugging at her hair, making it a riot of gold about her shoulders. She wore a blue cotton dress and as the wind pulled at the fabric the suggestion of a lovely body could be seen. I was young and impressed and I returned several times to admire the painting.'

'Perhaps it was the girl you admired and not just the artistic brush strokes,' Dinah interjected.

'I daresay it was.' Jason took a deep swallow of his wine. 'I know I wanted to possess the painting, but it was only on show in the gallery, part of an exhibition of new artistic work by British painters. Even the gallery didn't get to own it, because the artist never sold it. I'd say in retrospect that it was a girl he was madly in love with, perhaps a girl he'd lost to another man. Anyway, I never forgot his work, and when the notion came to me to have your portrait added to the family gallery I decided to get in touch with Sothern and he agreed to come and meet you. He informed me that he doesn't always accept a commission, even for a substantial fee, so I'd like you to be on your best behaviour, young woman.'

'I always am,' Dinah murmured, 'with other men.'

'How many other men do you know, my dear?'

'Well, there's Roger who does my hair at the Vogue salon. Then there's Fergus at the ice-cream parlour who always puts an extra cherry on my Creme Supreme—do you think he's trying to imply something?'

Jason gave an unexpected laugh. 'You're good company when you make the effort, Dinah. Eat up your rice pudding.'

'Jason, is it in Latin men to like fat women?' she queried.

'It could be, but I'm only quarter-part Latin.'

'Are you serious about having a portrait made of me, Jason?'

'Perfectly serious. I'd like Sothern to capture you on canvas the way he captured that other girl. She looked so alive and yet at the same time ethereal.'

'I shan't look ethereal for long,' Dinah grumbled, 'what with pregnancy and rice puddings!'

'I'm sure Sothern is clever enough to conceal any little bulges that might start to show.'

'Damn, I've got to get tubby while you stay looking like a—a matador!' She wiped her lips on the damask napkin. 'I know, why don't you sit for the portrait?'

'Don't talk nonsense, Dinah. You'll look quite fetching.'

'The painting of your mother is lovely,' Dinah reflected, 'and she was carrying you at the time, wasn't she?'

Jason nodded. 'It's a pity she wasn't a happier woman ... you can see the unhappiness in her eyes. But the girl in Sothern's painting was deeply involved with a man and it showed in the half-shy, half-awareness in the way she held her body. You felt she was in love, and Sothern entitled the painting *Domini*.'

'Do you suppose that was her name?' Dinah asked, intrigued.

'I rather fancy it was. She looked as if she might have an unusual kind of name for she certainly had a rare type of beauty, totally natural, with none of that cosmetic gloss about her, as if she had spent hours in the beauty salon before posing for her portrait. Sothern caught a mixture of patrician coolness and underlying passion.'

'Jason, you sound as if you fell madly in love with her!' Dinah said it with a laugh, but she was curious ... even slightly resentful that he could place that unknown girl on a pedestal.

'Would it matter to you if I did?' He scanned Dinah's face, his expression quizzical.

'It would make you seem more—human,' she retorted.

'I had no idea I was inhuman.'

'There are times when you seem to be.'

'Cold and stony, I suppose you mean?'

'Yes.'

'Isn't that a contradiction in terms? I thought what you hated about me was the fact that I turned out not to be a plaster saint.'

'Oh, you know very well what I mean, Jason.

You just don't take into account someone else's feelings.'

'How do you make that out?'

'Y-you took me against my will—that's what you did!'

'Sounds like a line from a Victorian melodrama,' he said dryly.

'You're simply evading the truth a-and turning things around to suit yourself!' Dinah said crossly.

'Am I really?' Jason took a look at the empty dish in front of her. 'Did you enjoy your pudding?'

'Yes, it was quite nice.'

'Now you get my point, sometimes the things we don't want turn out to be rather more pleasant than we expect.'

'Jason, how can you compare rice pudding to— to——' She broke off, colour sweeping into her face at what he outrageously implied . . . that being with him that night had been a pleasant experience when he knew very well that she had cried and clawed him, and felt shamed to the roots of her hair.

'You behaved like—like some savage out of a desert tent,' she said stormily.

'Did I?' A glimmer came into his eyes as he took in the confusion of her face. 'Put it down to my Moorish genes.'

'Oh, it's all very well for you to be flippant about it, but I was crazy with shame when I found out that I was going to have a baby because of you—I didn't know what to do, or who to turn to!'

'All you had to do was turn to me, Dinah.' His voice softened. 'I was always waiting for you to get in touch—you must have known that.'

'Contact you so you could feel pleased with your prowess? It was probably what you were waiting to hear, that you had a reason for tying me down. I—I begin to believe that you did it quite deliberately.'

'If you want to believe that, Dinah, then go ahead,' he said generously. 'If you want to turn me into the satyr of the season, then by all means do so. With some pregnant women it's plum jam or pickles, but with you it seems to be sour grapes.'

'Oh——' Dinah searched the table as if looking for an object to aim at him, 'I'd give anything to knock that smirk off your face!'

'Don't do it with the cut-glass,' he entreated. 'It's not only valuable, but I'd hate turning up at the bank with adhesive plaster adorning my face.'

'How did you explain away those scratches I gave you?'

'You don't imagine I went to work the next day, do you?' He widened his dark eyes at her and looked genuinely surprised that she should think he had. 'You'd vanished, Dinah. You'd run off God knows where and I was frantic to find you——'

'Did you think I'd jumped off the cliffs like that other poor girl?' Dinah wanted to know. 'Did you get the lifeboat men out to look for me?'

'As a matter of fact I did.'

'Really?' She studied him in a certain amazement. 'Was I that much on your conscience?'

'Yes, if you must know.'

'It didn't occur to me to drown myself,' she said reflectively. 'I wonder why?'

'You like being alive too much, Dinah. You've always been a vibrant child.'

'I'm no more a child, Jason. By the way, Dr Malcolm mentioned that she'd like to come to dinner one evening. I believe she's inquisitive about us, and she thinks you're madly attractive and that I'm a very fortunate girl to have you.'

'So you are.' He pushed back his chair and came round to where she sat, pulling her to her feet and tucking her hand through the crook of his arm. 'We'll take coffee in the music room, and then I'll play to you—it soothes you.'

'And in the process soothes the valuable child. Do we invite the doctor to dinner, Jason?'

'I've already done so, when she telephoned to tell me you'd sailed through your check-up and we could expect to have a healthy baby if you make an effort to eat all those nourishing dinners Leon is going to cook for you.'

'I notice you've been spreading the word that you're going to be a father regardless of the fact that people can count—don't you care what people think of me, Jason?'

'This isn't the nineteenth century, dear heart, as you pointed out to me when you talked so blithely of visiting that clinic.'

'I—I wasn't feeling blithe,' she admitted, 'and I would prefer you not to use those endearments that mean so little. Your class does have such a habit of doing so!'

'My class, Dinah?' He glanced down at her. 'Don't forget that your mother was vaguely related to my mother.'

Dinah wore a thoughtful expression. 'I wish I looked like her; my father always referred to her eyes as being cornflower blue, and her hair had a lovely deep wave in it.'

'Each person has something of note, Dinah. You have a husky little catch in your voice, and your ankles are very eye-catching.'

'Then I shall have to remember to show them off when Barry Sothern paints me—when do I get to meet the great artist?'

'On Sunday evening. He'll be dining with us along with the lady doctor.'

'Good, I shall be able to ask him all about the girl named Domini.'

'That might not be wise.' Jason frowned. 'There are men who don't like to talk about their love, least of all to a stranger.'

'Oh, I don't know, sometimes it's easier to talk to a stranger about personal things. Ships passing in the night and all that.'

'Perhaps you're right, Dinah.' They entered the handsome music room where coffee was brought to them, and Jason played for her the Beethoven piano sonata, more popularly called *Pathétique*. Dinah had always loved it and Jason played with a sure yet sensitive touch which made her think of other evenings and other days, when she was home from school and he thought of ways to make her holidays enjoyable.

London visits to his favourite restaurants,

picnics on the beach, and sometimes a play or a concert intended to broaden her mind, though the plays he chose were never stuffy. She had loved musicals such as *My Fair Lady*. The Cinderella story had appealed to her ... but in those days she had been a romantic at heart and had believed in the story of the worldly man who shaped a little nobody into a lady.

Dinah sighed as Jason wandered into the Liszt *Liebestraum*. What she had found out was that Jason was two people in one body; the cultured man of the world concealing a more savage inner being. Her hand clenched against her side where his child was growing day by day, sharing her blood and marrow but bound to be a Devrel because Jason was so dominant, not only in ways but in looks.

She watched him through a blur, having taken off her glasses and laid them on the coffee table. She saw the rise and fall of his hands on the keys of the piano ... those well-shaped hands which had subdued her body and made her respond to him even as her mind rejected every kiss and every caress which led to a wild culmination whose recollection made her heart hammer in her breast.

She could hear herself breathing, her lips slightly open and moist. Beneath her hand she could feel the tautness of her breast, its peak thrusting forward to strain the opal silk of her dress. By contrast her limbs felt languorous, quite unable to stir when Jason came over to her, the music at an end.

He stood gazing down at her, then he sank down so his knees enclosed her on the carpet. His hand moved and he pushed his long fingers through her hair.

'You should have been a concert pianist,' she told him in a husky voice. 'You have the single-hearted dedication that it takes.'

He shook his head. 'I wanted to dedicate myself to something else.'

'Banking?'

He didn't reply. He was leaning towards her, studying her face as if fascinated by something in it other people didn't seem to see. His eyes were dark ... dark like the night beyond the ivory curtained windows.

'Dinah?' His voice was deep ... deep like a drowning pool. 'My dear child ...' His touch moved down her body to her hand, brushing it away so he could encircle her breast with his fingers. Then lowering his head he let his warm lips touch her through the opal silk.

She gave a little gasp. 'You mustn't——'

'You said that before and look what happened.' His hand unclosed the chain about her waist and the rosewood clock ticked softly on the mantel above them, merging with the slither of silk as Jason drew it down until it pooled at her feet.

She lay there on the carpet in a single flimsy garment, her spine arching over his arm as he raised her until their lips were a bare inch apart. 'Sweet,' he murmured. 'No one knows you as I do, Dinah.'

Her eyes closed as their lips met ... then

wildly, wildly she thrust him away from her.
'Don't—I won't have you touch me—I hate you!'

Every muscle in him seemed to go tense, then
he drew away from her and rose to his feet. He
walked over to the windows and stood there with
his back to her. In a while he said harshly: 'I
should have guessed, shouldn't I?'

'Guessed what, Jason?' She lay there unmov-
ing, feeling a strange mixture of feelings and
unable to sort them out.

'You allowed me just within reach just to prove
something, didn't you?'

'And what have I proved, Jason?'

'That desire is possible between us but not
permissible!'

'I don't understand what you're saying.'

'Don't you?' He swung round, fingers thrusting
through his hair. 'We can never be indifferent to
each other because of Hallowe'en night . . . if I
hadn't touched you that night, I might have you
right now. But I have to pay—we both have to
pay, and the price is high. Let's hope you don't
keep adding to it until I run out of emotional
revenue!'

'You—you're talking in riddles.' She sat up,
clutching her dress to her body. 'What do you
mean by emotional revenue?'

'When you've grown up a little more, Dinah,
you may work out the answer for yourself.' He
walked past her, adding in a frozen voice,
'Goodnight, child. Put on your dress before you
come upstairs or the staff might assume that we
enjoy being married to each other!'

As the door closed behind him Dinah realised that tears were creeping down her face.

CHAPTER SIX

JASON told Dinah to go and buy herself a new dress for the dinner party on Sunday evening; something really stunning.

'No expense spared?' she queried, as they sat at breakfast on Saturday morning.

He lowered his newspaper and studied her in a ray of sunlight, for the weather had brightened and most of the snow had melted away overnight. Birds were chattering in the trees and the morning room had a bright aspect, a window standing ajar to let in the sound and smell of the sea.

That bright ray of sunlight stroked through Dinah's hair, and it had a young soft look, and as Jason looked at her sitting there, buttering a piece of toast, a kind of perplexity moved in his eyes.

'Buy the best in the shop,' he said generously. 'Do you know, there are times when you look a schoolgirl again.'

'I don't particularly feel like one,' she rejoined. 'Half an hour ago I was feeling sick, but Hester has the remedy. She makes me sip distilled water and with it I have to nibble a plain biscuit.'

'Does it work—it appears to?' he said.

She nodded. 'Hester is so sensible without being in the least boring; we get along fine.'

'I'm glad you're friends. Her father is a guard at the bank.'

Dinah crunched her toast and nodded as Jason lifted the coffee pot, watching as he refilled her cup, adding at least an inch of cream to it. 'Do you think it's a good idea that I buy a new dress—I shall soon be bursting its seams?'

'I want you to impress Barry Sothern,' he said frankly.

'You're really keen on that painting, aren't you?' Dinah peered at him through her spectacles, at half-mast on her small nose. 'Is the portrait to be put among your souvenirs?'

'If you want to put it that way.' He folded his newspaper and lounged back in his chair, sipping coffee, long legs stretched forward. 'You won't mind if he agrees to accept the commission, will you? I don't know how many sittings an artist such as Sothern requires, but he'll be informed that you're expecting my child. I don't want the sittings to exhaust you.'

'Oh, I'm fit enough, and look, Jason, I'm eating for two.' She exhibited a second slice of toast piled with marmalade. 'Dr Malcolm was mainly concerned about my nerves, but I couldn't tell her, could I, why my nerves are in a bit of a state.'

'Meaning that I'm the one who makes you nervous, Dinah?' His eyes were intent upon her, fresh-skinned and quite without make-up, her hair scooped back and tied with a shoelace.

'It can't be helped, I suppose.' She gave a shrug. 'You and I are oil and water and we just don't mix—not as husband and wife.'

He finished his coffee and broodingly watched

the antics of a striped honey-bee forcing its way
into the cup of a flower; they were cut in the
greenhouse and placed in vases around the house,
and often bees came in with them, for Tyson the
gardener also kept bees and a pot of the honey
was on the breakfast table.

Suddenly the petals of the reluctant flower
sprang open and the bee slithered inside, emitting
a triumphant buzzing as he plundered the pollen.

Jason abruptly shifted his gaze to Dinah. 'We
haven't talked about what happened the other
evening—was that oil and water?'

Again she shrugged and licked marmalade
from her finger. 'Do we have to talk about it?'

'You invited what almost happened.'

'N-not consciously,' she denied.

His brows drew together, forming a black bar
above the bold line of his nose. Beneath those
brows his eyes were impenetrable, for he had his
back to the sunlight.

'Do I assume that subconsciously you would
like it to happen?'

'Is it so important, Jason?' All at once she
could feel her heart pounding beneath her casual
shirt and a potent little quiver went through her,
placing its dart at the apex of her body. The
screen of her mind held images of herself arched
over Jason's strong arm, her hair flowing over his
hands, her lips opened to the demanding warmth
of his.

'Was it just a game, Dinah? A little teasing
game you thought up—if it was, my girl, then
I'm warning you not to play it too often. The

next time you might get more than you bargained for!'

'I wasn't playing a game—I was half asleep, you know music does that to me—ouch!' She jumped to her feet as something jabbed her, then saw on the wing a tiger-gold honey-bee. 'That brute stung me!'

'Let me see.' Jason strode round to her, took her slim arm in his fingers and examined a red mark plain against her white skin. Abruptly he bent his head and she felt the edge of his teeth as he sucked her arm, then he turned his head and wiped his mouth on his handkerchief.

'The sting is out,' he said. 'We'll go upstairs and put some antiseptic on the arm.'

He walked her across the hall with his arm slung about her waist and she gave a sudden laugh. 'Jason, it was a bee sting, not a snakebite!'

'All the same, it needs to be treated.' He marched her along the upstairs gallery and before she could protest she found herself in his bedroom and he was fetching the bottle of antiseptic from his bathroom.

Dinah glanced around her, rooms she hadn't ventured into since she began to grow up . . . now she was actually his wife, and her gaze rested on the great oaken bed with the tall posts and the burned-gold coverlet whose folds hung to the thick rugs at either side of the bed. His range of closets were of carved oak; Jason had always liked good clothes and she knew there were many fine, well-tailored suits and more casual ensembles in his closets.

There on the bureau was the leather box stamped with his initials in which he kept his collection of cuff-links, watches and shirt studs. There were military hairbrushes ranged side by side, and the gold-framed photograph of herself on her graduation from college.

She went to the bureau and picked up the photograph, studying the girl in the college gown and cap, a vagrant smile clinging to her lips.

She gave a start and almost dropped the frame as Jason came and stood behind her, studying the photograph over her shoulder. 'I—I was thinking how young I look,' she said, a trifle nervously.

'You haven't changed all that much—didn't I say so at breakfast?'

Dinah replaced the frame on the bureau and felt the quick beating of her heart as he took her arm in his fingers. 'Get ready for another sting,' he said, as he applied the damp cotton-wool to her skin.

But Dinah didn't feel anything, for she was too busy being conscious of his closeness; he wore a smart suit because he was going to the bank to discuss business. When he had to meet members of the board he always dressed in a sober way, dark blue this morning with a very fine, close stripe in the material. There was a fine, dark blue stripe in his shirt, and his tie was impeccably knotted.

Dinah breathed *L'homme est rare*, with its tang of woody spiciness, and she was intensely aware of what linked them, the baby that lay inside her.

Jason's baby! Still the realisation could give her

a sense of shock . . . he had been her guardian since she was a schoolgirl and adjusting to their new relationship was difficult.

He had attended her graduation and her classmates had followed him with their eyes, tall and dark and distinguished. When she had walked around the grounds with him that sunny afternoon she had little dreamed that within six months she would be carrying his child.

'There, has it stopped hurting?' He caught her gaze upon his face and quirked an eyebrow quizzically.

'It didn't really hurt all that much—not the way other things have hurt me.'

His eyes narrowed. 'We're like a pair of dancers trapped in a spotlight,' he mused. 'We go round and round to the same old tune, don't we?'

Her breath caught. 'Why—oh, why did things have to change?'

'You grew up,' he said quietly. 'You were no longer a schoolgirl in my house but a young woman——'

'So you proposed to me,' she broke in, 'knowing that if I went on living in your house some people would—imply things.'

He inclined his dark head. 'When you came to me, you were a kid in a pot hat and tunic. But as it says in the song, little girls grow up in the most alarming way . . . I thought it best that we marry.'

'And I didn't ask questions until those two women——' Dinah broke off and looked around her in a slightly dazed way. Her reflection was caught in his wall mirror and she stared at herself, a still very slim figure in casual shirt and jeans, her hair drawn back from her face, the harlequin spectacles perched on her nose. She raised a hand and pushed them into place.

'I'll never look like your girl in the painting,' she said. 'The girl Domini, with the wild gold hair. Mr Sothern will have to be a genius to make me look anything!'

'Stop that!' Jason took her by the shoulders and forced her to look at him. 'I admired Sothern's painting for the life and vibrancy in it, not merely for the girl's beauty——'

'All the same, she was beautiful,' Dinah broke in, 'and if there's one thing I've learned about you, Jason, it's that you like things of beauty. Why did you have to twist up our lives by playing the gentleman and asking me to marry you? That's what started all this! Was it because—yes, I believe the real motive for your proposal was that you didn't like my suggestion that I look for a job like Cissie Lang. You had it stamped through your brain that I was the helpless child in the pot hat who'd get trampled on if she ventured outside your jurisdiction.'

She flung back her head and the blue storm light blazed in her eyes. 'I wouldn't have come to much harm working at Grady's store—it was here in your house that I got into trouble!'

His fingers gripped to the point of pain when she said that, and for several seconds they were face to face like combatants in the arena, intent on wounding each other.

Slowly Jason's fingers relaxed and they both knew that he had left bruises beneath the fabric of her shirt. Dinah drew away from him and said coldly:

'Don't bother to wait to drive me into town. I've got to get ready and I'll take half an hour at least. I wouldn't want you to be late for your board meeting.'

'As I'm the general manager, everyone waits for me. Of course I'll wait and drive you to the dress shop. I'd appreciate the company.'

And when he said those words, and before she could stop herself, Dinah glanced towards his king-sized bed. He gave a curt laugh, bringing a flush into her cheeks.

'Not there, my dear. I'd need more than half an hour for what you have in mind.'

'What I——?' Her flush deepened furiously. 'I—I'll go and get ready.'

She fled away from him, hastening along the wide panelled gallery to her own set of rooms. She flung the door shut behind her and felt herself breathing quickly. She stood still for a few moments, her hands pressed to her hot cheeks. *Calm down*, she told herself, this kind of emotional behaviour wasn't good for her, the doctor had warned her of that. But whenever she and Jason were together she seemed to lose her poise, and the atmosphere between them was always charged with threat ... they were like a pair of tigers in a cage, prowling around each other and hoping to be the first to lash out.

Dinah walked across to the shelves where her

collection of tigers was arranged; she picked up the one Jason had bought her that morning at Grady's. She raised it as if to hurl it and smash it ... tiger, tiger, eyes alight in the shadows, muscles rippling beneath its pelt, breath hot and devouring.

Her hand was shaking as it placed the tiger back among its companions, then slipping out of her shirt and jeans she changed into a blue linen dress with a blouson jacket. She briskly brushed her hair, dabbed on face powder from the cut-glass bowl, added colour to her lips and sprayed on *Arpège*. She was fetching her shoes from the closet when Hester tapped on the bedroom door and came in.

'Miss, you should have rung for me!' Hester looked quite put out, as if Dinah was already cumbersome and in dire need of assistance.

Dinah gave a cynical little laugh. 'I shan't need helping into my clothes for quite some time, so don't look so anxious! I'm well aware that the lord and master has given you orders to cater to my every wish, and to ensure that I don't lift a hairbrush from one side of the dressing-table to the other, but that's because he's anxious to be a proud father; it isn't because he adores me!'

Dinah flung round to face the mirror and unsparingly studied her reflection. 'What an idea! No wonder we get curious looks when we go into town together ... the catch of the county in tandem with a girl in glasses!'

'Miss Dinah, you shouldn't talk like that,' Hester exclaimed. 'Sir married you, so he must——'

'Sir *had* to marry me.' Dinah turned to face the girl, a defiant light in her eyes. 'I might not be the catch of the season, but he's no knight in shining armour, take it from me!'

'Miss Dinah, he tells us all to take good care of you, when he's away for the day at the bank.'

'Only because I'm the incubator for his precious infant!' Dinah patted her body where there was a slight but definite increase in the curve of her stomach. 'It's the baby he cares about, Hester. I'm carrying the Devrel heir and that's why everyone is given orders to take care of me. Did you imagine, Hester, that he's in love with me?'

Dinah gave an off-key laugh as she slipped into her shoes and picked up her handbag. 'I know you devour those old Hollywood movies on the telly, and you probably think that my dear husband is just like one of those tall, dark and fascinating film stars, who at the end of the movie takes the girl passionately into his arms and tells her she's divine. Divine—me?'

Dinah was still laughing to herself as she walked downstairs to where Jason waited in the hall, halfway through a cheroot. He stubbed it in a brass tray when she appeared and came to the foot of the staircase, holding out a hand to her. She deliberately avoided it by skipping around him, throwing back over her shoulder as she made for the door:

'I've just been telling Hester that I don't want people fussing over me. I'm not going to fall down the stairs even if I do need glasses!'

She walked out to the car and saw that he was driving the Jaguar today, a dark gold cat of a car in the sunlight, long and powerful.

'You like gold, don't you, Jason?' she said.

'An appropriate colour for a banker, wouldn't you say?' He opened the passenger door for her.

'Let me drive?' Dinah turned a persuasive look upon him. 'I enjoy driving and I promise not to go mad.'

He shook his head. 'What's under that bonnet isn't for little girls to play with.'

'Chauvinist brute!' With her mouth gone sulky Dinah slid into the passenger seat. Jason came round and seated himself beside her, slamming the door, buckling his belt and starting the car. 'Belt up, Dinah.'

She did so as they swept smoothly down the drive, dappled by the shadows of trees and shrubs lining its long length to the main road. Dinah pressed a button and the window beside her slid down to let a gust of sea air into the car.

'What unpredictable weather we have in this country,' she remarked. 'It snows one day, then fools the birds into thinking that spring is coming.'

'It isn't so far off,' he said, adding quietly: 'I'm not being a taskmaster, child, but you know there've been accidents on this road, and I don't want you involved in one. I was at the scene of one accident recently—the car slammed down into the ravine and the driver—a woman—was badly smashed up. She died on the way to hospital.'

'And if that happened to me, I'd probably take the precious baby with me.' Dinah watched him from the corner of her eye, awaiting his reaction; his jaw tightened so the muscle took definition.

'You will take the view that I'm bullying you, Dinah, but it isn't always so.'

'Only most times,' she murmured. 'You really assume that you know what is best for me and everyone else, don't you?'

'Put it down to practice,' he drawled. 'I've had to be a corporation boss since I was about your age—oh, I knew I owed it to the Devrel tradition to make merchant banking my life's work and there has to be a man at the top, someone who can take the credit for ideas that work, and accept the whip when something goes wrong. Like on a ship, there's only one skipper.'

'Like in a marriage, there's only one boss.' As she spoke Dinah fiddled with her seatbelt and eased it a little. 'I am getting fat, you know!'

'It becomes you,' he soothed, 'and it won't be for a lifetime. Hold on to that and let it be your thought for the day.'

'Beastly men,' she exclaimed, 'getting all the perks and none of the pricks!'

'That, my dear, is very close to what is called a *double entendre*,' he drawled.

'What a mind you have, Jason!'

'Aren't you amused by a little improper wit, Dinah?'

She thought over his words and a smile brushed her lips. Some of the conversation at college had been amusingly salacious at times;

some of the girls had been wildly interested in
men and open in their expectations; a few had
already started to explore the mystery ... but
Dinah had never dreamed that her initiation
would be in Jason's hands.

As they drove on she gazed at his hands on the
wheel of the Jaguar, firmly in control of the
power under the sleek bonnet. She began to be
aware of her own breathing again and the feel of
his leg near her own, firm-muscled under the
dark blue material. For a man in his late thirties
Jason had kept his body like whipcord, and a
kind of animal magnetism seemed to exude
through the burnt-cinnamon skin that lay sleek
against the muscle and bone of him.

He was so masculine and yet at the same time a
very complex human being; certainly one Dinah
didn't attempt to understand. The deep secret
centre of his personality was like a concealed
room that she felt tempted to explore, yet in
which she was afraid of being locked.

'Shall I drop you off at Maison Teri?' he asked,
as they entered the town centre, where the shops
and offices were in contrast to the surrounding
countryside which was very picturesque.

'Please. Do you think I should have something
done about my hair—have it cut or waved?'

As he pulled into the kerb in front of the dress
shop he turned to study her. 'Leave your hair
exactly as it is, in that casual style. I'm convinced
that Barry Sothern is an artist who prefers
naturalness to artificiality, and you have the kind
of face that doesn't need an elaborate hairstyle.'

'Meaning that I'm plain.'

'Meaning that you're real and touchable and not some made-up little madam on the front of a magazine,' he said crisply. Abruptly he leaned forward and his lips closed over hers, so startling her that her lips lay open beneath his. He placed a hand at the back of her head and held the kiss for several long moments, until involuntarily her hands clenched his shoulders.

Slowly he let her go and her lip colouring was on his mouth. She fumbled her bag open and handed him a tissue. 'You'd best wipe your mouth, unless you want your fellow directors to think you wear make-up!'

He drew the tissue across his lips and studied the colour that lay across her cheekbones, a natural flush showing through her fine skin. 'Meet me on the harbour for lunch. Both of us should be through with our business by one o'clock.'

Dinah nodded and slid from the Jaguar. She closed the door and watched it glide away in the direction of the bank, which occupied an entire corner facing the harbour, where the sound of seagulls could be heard, rising gracefully against the high cliffs that sheltered the town, then swooping down to skim the sea that beat against the harbour's cobbled walls.

Dinah took a deep breath of the air. This was what she had missed in London, the fresh and invigorating smell of the ocean, and that special lightness in the atmosphere which the heavy and perpetual city traffic turned to a smell of fumes.

In a while she walked across the pavement to the swing doors of *Maison Teri*, feeling a tremor in her legs ... a tremor perhaps occasioned by the kiss which Jason had insisted upon. She would never understand him ... never know what it was he really wanted of her.

Was possession all he was capable of feeling?

Dinah believed so ... his possession of her had become such a habit that he couldn't relate to her other than as the man who had taken charge of her when she was a small girl, a shy stranger in his house, with no one else in the world to turn to. Had he not been there, then she would have been consigned to an orphanage, to grow up among other deprived youngsters.

Instead here she stood, in the foyer of an expensive dress establishment, being approached by a saleslady who was all smiles for a customer with a wealthy husband.

'Good morning, Mrs Devrel. How very nice to see you!'

She was acceptable to these people because she was Jason Devrel's wife, even though in secret they might be amazed that he should want her ... the little orphan in glasses.

Teri Lennox was in the showroom when Dinah entered, and they greeted each other warmly. Dinah admired Teri, who was a dedicated career woman in her middle thirties, and striking to look at with her scorched-gold hair, sculptured cheekbones and elegant figure. Teri had been a highly successful model who had wisely invested her savings in fashion. She had gone to Paris for

two years and been taught how to cut and design
by one of the French masters. The rumour was
that she had fallen in love with him, but he had
turned out to be a dedicated bachelor.

On her return to England, Teri had put
romance behind her and used her energies to
create her own line in fashion. She had worked
hard, well equipped with zest and charm, and her
shop had soon become a Mecca for the
fashionable women of Havenshore.

Dinah had been a client since she was eighteen
and her measurements were kept here. Today,
she told herself ruefully, those measurements
would have to be discarded for new ones.

'My dear girl!' Teri caught Dinah to her and
kissed her on both cheeks in the French way. 'I
congratulate you, you've landed the biggest prize
in the West Country.'

'I'm glad you think so.' Dinah couldn't keep a
quiet note of irony out of her voice. Because Teri
was going to insist on showing her a selection of
dresses in her style and measurements, Dinah
was going to have to break the news about the
baby that was burgeoning under her waistline.

Teri looked her over, saying warmly: 'It's good
to see you, Di. Your face has an interesting
thinness, but your figure—my dear, is it a little
fuller than it used to be?'

'I'm afraid it is.' Dinah took a deep breath.
'Jason and I are expecting an addition to the
family.'

'You don't say so?' Teri blinked her skilfully
made up eyelashes. 'But I'd heard that you only

tied the knot last month—the pair of you lost precious little time, but how can you be so sure?'

'In the usual way.' Dinah felt herself flushing under her friend's regard. 'I have my baby in August, right at the beginning.'

'I—see.' Surprise flashed in Teri's eyes. 'I never took you for a naughty girl, which means that it has to be real old-fashioned love that swept the pair of you off your feet. Am I right?'

Dinah shrugged diffidently.

'I bet Jason is thrilled?'

'You could say that.' Dinah spoke rather pertly. 'He thinks this baby is going to be about the most wonderful creature that ever got born. I'm amazed at how much he wants to be a parent.'

'It's to be expected, Di. He needs a son to carry on the Devrel name and all that goes with it, and you have to remember that he was an only child who probably experienced loneliness when he was young. Rich kids don't get to play in the streets, where the rough and tumble of life can be enjoyed. Do you know, I always had the feeling Jason was training you to be his wife, and I remember how when he brought you to me, he insisted that I keep your style as simple as possible. Have you still got that rather gothic dress I designed for you? It made you look like a girl who was kept in a tower.'

'Spectacles and all?' Dinah murmured.

Teri gave a laugh. 'Di, they're part of your persona, and they always look rather touching on your nose. Don't mind them. I know a few slinky models who deliberately wear them because they look sexy. That old Dorothy Parker cliché died out with the dodo, and the new generation accept that girls in specs have lots of sex.'

'Is having sex so very important?' Dinah asked, remembering the slither of silk as Jason unpeeled it from her body, beneath which she had worn a slip to match that gothic-styled dress. Jason had wanted her . . . wanted her because his baby was inside her, intensifying that possessive streak in him.

'Making love is important,' Teri murmured, a tinge of sadness in her eyes. Then she took Dinah by the hand and drew her to one of the fitting cubicles. 'I'm going to have to take your new measurements, even though they won't stay stable for long. What are you hoping for, a boy or a girl?'

'Jason wants a son.' Dinah slipped out of her jacket and dress. 'I'm hoping it will be a boy, because life is less tough on the male of the species.'

'Except when there's a war.' Teri drew a tape measure around Dinah's hips and jotted down the figures. Then she moved the tape upwards and suddenly gave a whistle. 'Your bust, Di, has increased by more than an inch—is that good news?'

Dinah pulled a face. 'I feel as if I'm going to look like a barrel! As I told Jason, men wouldn't be so fond of a good time if they had to produce the children.'

'True,' Teri smiled, 'but it's shared pleasure,

even if the guy doesn't have to become a roly-poly, and I'm pretty darned sure Jason is good to you. I bet he spoils you, doesn't he?'

'I—I suppose he does.' Dinah smiled reluctantly. 'He wants me to have something really special for a dinner party we're giving on Sunday evening ... have you something that will make me look glamorous?'

'As it happens,' Teri looked thoughtful, 'I do have an exclusive that was ordered by a client who was very much your size. I'm afraid she had an accident a few weeks ago and she didn't survive it. If you're superstitious, Di, then we'll forget it, but it's a dream of a dress and I just know the colour will become you. I did consider destroying the dress, but it would be such a shame—do you want me to show it to you?'

Dinah stood biting her lip. 'The woman who ordered it, was she killed on the ravine road?'

Teri nodded. 'Her car skidded over the edge; it was a sports model and she was thrown out, poor thing.'

'Jason saw the accident,' Dinah told her.

'I say, that couldn't have been pleasant for him!'

'He refuses to let me drive because of it. I wonder what he'd say——' Dinah broke off, her slender brows drawn together in thought.

'Let's forgot it,' Teri said briskly. 'Put it down to designer's vanity that I hated the thought of the dress never being worn. I'll destroy it——'

'No, I'd like to see it,' Dinah broke in. 'What colour is it?'

'A very ethereal shade of grey-blue, and the fabric is divine. Are you sure you want me to fetch it?'

'Yes.' Dinah had made up her mind. 'Why be superstitious about fate; things happen to us, they aren't planned by the dark powers—are they?'

'Who knows? I'll go and fetch the dress; shan't be a tick.'

Teri left Dinah alone in the cubicle, with exotic flowers woven in silk thread in the curtains. There was a little satin stool and she sat down in her slip and waited for Teri to return with the dress whose owner had met such a tragic end. Dinah wanted to try it on, perversely wanting it so she could savour Jason's reaction when she told him about its history.

The cubicle curtains swept open and Teri came in, carrying in a plastic cover the flowing skirted dress.

Dinah stood up and watched as the dress was revealed, and she caught her breath at its loveliness. 'Isn't the colour exactly right for you?' Teri enthused. 'Are you still game to try it on, or have you had second thoughts?'

Dinah stroked the skirt and the tips of her fingers seemed to tingle, as if the lustrous fabric was charged with a life of its own. 'Is it very expensive?' she asked.

'Jason can afford it,' Teri assured her. 'Now let's see if it fits you.'

It did, and in the mirrored rotunda Dinah saw herself from all angles in the dress; the bodice encased her like a shining skin and the skirt flowed to the floor in a cascade of luxurious silk. When she moved the dress moved with her and it made a whispering sound.

'It's very beautiful,' she murmured. 'Does it look too grand for me?'

'The colour blends with your eyes,' said Teri, a note of satisfaction in her voice, for she was the designer and it was pleasing on Dinah. 'I'm going to tell you something, my girl, a lot of women come and go through my doors, but I've never seen one of them with skin like yours. What an advert you'd make for skin lotion!'

Dinah flushed, too modest to ever imagine that she had attributes other women might envy. 'I've been called an Orphan Annie in glasses,' she said ruefully, 'but never an advert for skin lotion.'

'Don't tell me Jason's made love to you and not remarked on your satiny skin?' Teri had a twinkle in her eyes. 'He has, hasn't he?'

Dinah lowered her gaze and swirled in the dress, listening to the silken fabric. 'You're a romantic, Teri. You should think about getting married yourself.'

'The trouble is, Di, I like being my own boss and seeing my business expand and grow successful. I don't know if I could combine that with being a wife. I have this idea, you see, that you give all to love if you're a woman, or you give it to your work. I bet Jason's a super husband, isn't he? In all the important ways?'

'I suppose you mean—romantically?'

'Yes, taking charge in a masterful way but

caring that you're a person as well as a wife. Or have I read him wrong?'

'You've only read half the book,' Dinah said quietly. 'Like most people, there's more to Jason than meets the eye. We've all got a public face and a private one, haven't we?'

'And thank heaven for it,' Teri said fervently. 'Look at my image—here in the shop I have to be wise, elegant and in command, but it feels so good when I get home and can relax. I scrub off all the make-up, take off my girdle and tuck into a good thick pizza. I love the taste of cheese and peppers on my mouth instead of lip colouring. I like walking about in bare feet, and I like to let my hair down. But who would believe it when I'm here in charge of the shop?'

'You are elegance personified,' Dinah smiled.

'You're elegant yourself in that dress, Di. Well, have I sold it to you, or do you want to look at some others?'

'No, I want this one.' Not for very much longer would she be able to look so sleek, and Dinah could see that the colour became her, reflecting as it did the blended blue and grey of her eyes.

'I'm not going to think about that poor woman who should have had it.' She stroked the silk down over her hips. 'I'll take it, and you can send the account to Jason.'

'Only too pleased to do so.' Teri helped Dinah off with the dress and carefully replaced it in its cover. 'I'll have it delivered to your house this afternoon, and I'm betting Jason will love you in it.'

Dinah smiled faintly at the thought. 'You're very romantic for a career woman, Teri. I begin to wonder myself if romance is going out of people, leaving them with too much realism to cope with. It makes people hard, don't you think? I—I worry in case I'm getting hard-boiled.'

'You look soft-boiled to me, honey.' Teri gave Dinah a steady look. 'I can imagine Jason shutting out the world when he's alone with you—am I right?'

'Well, we are rather isolated, up there on Devrel Drive,' Dinah said evasively. Inwardly as she buttoned her jacket something was hurting ... if only it were all true, what Teri Lennox believed of her marriage!

Enwrapped in her thoughts, Dinah made her way down to the harbour where Jason was leaning on the cobbled wall, admiring a pair of swans on a sandbank, their graceful necks entwined.

'Beautiful creatures, aren't they?' he said, when he became aware that Dinah had quietly joined him. 'Did the fittings go well, and did you acquire a stunning gown?'

Her mouth gave a little wry twist when he spoke of the gown she had chosen to buy. 'Yes, Teri was in good spirits.'

'Good. Look at those birds, graceful as ballet dancers!'

'Jason, for a man who admires the beauties of nature, you chose strangely when you married me!'

He turned at once to face her ... she was

shivering slightly, having left her topcoat in the car. He caught at her hands and began to chafe them. 'Dammit, Dinah, why do you keep harping on that theme? We're married, so let's leave it at that!'

She studied him, tall and vigorous, his Latin heritage in his well-structured face and in his grace of bodily movement. 'Lord help the son and heir if he takes after me and is born myopic,' she said. 'At school we get called Four-eyes, did you know that?'

'I know, Dinah. Children can be unkind to each other, but without real malice.'

'Adults do it as well, Jason, only they do it with malice aforethought.'

'Why all this self-doubting?' he asked. 'Why does it have to matter if you aren't a bold-eyed blonde?'

'Matter?' she murmured. 'You—you might——'

She swallowed the word, and at once his eyes grew fierce.

'I might *what*? Don't leave me to guess, Dinah—come on!'

'You might—respect me.' Then she pulled free of him and walked quickly towards the nearby Kingfisher Restaurant where they were lunching.

'Do hurry,' she threw back at him. 'It's beginning to turn cold again.'

She heard his footfalls on the pavement behind her, then his hand was beneath her elbow, easing her hurried pace. 'Don't dash along like a whippet, you might stumble and fall over these old paving stones.'

'And do damage to your precious child?'

His fingers gripped and he brought her to a pause in the entrance of the restaurant. His eyes searched her face. 'Did Teri Lennox have something to say about your condition?' he demanded.

'Teri was thrilled, as a matter of fact.'

'Then why all the temperament?'

'Because I'm not thrilled,' she said defiantly. 'In your darned arrogance you expect me to be, but you—you've messed up my life, just as I was settled in a job I liked.'

'I daresay Grady's will take you back,' he said, his eyes and voice flinty. 'You talk about me respecting you—I don't know if I can respect someone who can't wait to run out on her child!'

'Oh——' Dinah caught her breath sharply, for a dart of pain had gone right through her. 'You have a cruel tongue, when you like, Jason!'

'*Touché*,' he said, and marched her into the dining-room of the Kingfisher, where they lunched with the minimum of conversation. Afterward he sent her home in a cab, where she sat silently in a corner, the defiance drained out of her eyes, leaving them lonely and sad.

When the cab swept past the ravine where the woman in the sports car had been fatally injured, Dinah caught her lip between her teeth and wondered if she would dare to wear the dress when the time came ... the dress of shadowy grey and blue.

Was there a curse on such things?

CHAPTER SEVEN

BARRY SOTHERN was a lion-like man, his strong brow thatched by a mane of silvery hair. He had a very attractive speaking voice shaded by a hint of working-class background; his hands were large and sure.

He sat beside Dinah at the dining-table and she couldn't help but be aware that he kept studying her, obviously to assess her appeal to him in a professional sense. She wondered what he was thinking as he ran his sorrel eyes over her hair and profile.

Rita Malcolm, looking extremely smart in a deep jade dress with a sleeveless jacket, sat chatting to Jason, so this made Dinah all the more conscious of Barry Sothern's scrutiny of herself.

'Do you want to have your portrait painted, Mrs Devrel?' he asked her suddenly, glancing a moment at Jason, as if suspecting that it was mainly the wish of a rich man to have his wife's likeness hung on his walls among other women who had married into the Devrel family.

Dinah spooned her avocado with shrimp and gave a slight shrug. 'I do as Jason wants,' she replied. 'His staff does the work around the house and he has a chef in the kitchen, so there's little for me to do except await the arrival of our baby.'

'And when will that be?' His eyes kindled into

a smile and she felt herself warming to his rugged personality.

'At the beginning of August, if all goes well.' She crossed her fingers. 'Ours is a Hallowe'en baby, so I'm hoping it won't be a witch or a warlock!'

'Are you superstitious?' He smiled as he spoke, as if he thought her very young ... obviously much younger than her husband, for Jason in evening wear always looked distinguished and on the edge of being severe. Somehow the dark suiting intensified his chiselled features, and in contrast Barry Sothern was rather like a weathered Roman statue.

'You should ask my husband that question, Mr Sothern. I'm quite certain that as an artist you can see shades of the desert in his face.'

The artist took an appreciative swallow of his wine. Then he leaned forward in a confidential way. 'I'd rather like to do a portrait of him as well,' he told her.

'In robes and head ropes?' she murmured.

A smile travelled over the craggy face and lit the sorrel eyes. 'You realise that I've decided to go ahead with your portrait, Mrs Devrel?'

'I thank you, Mr Sothern. Will you require me to dress up?'

His gaze ran over her. 'I may decide to paint you in the dress you're wearing; the colour is becoming and reflects the grey and blue of your eyes. You have an unusual kind of persona, if I may say so? Something elusive ... something the Irish probably have a word for—is it fey?'

Dinah flushed slightly. She realised that it probably wasn't unusual for an artist to speak in such a way, but Barry Sothern was very much a man and Dinah was aware of the sad, lonely area within herself that might respond to a man who was *simpatico*.

'Doesn't it disappoint you, Mr Sothern, that I don't look anything like the girl called Domini; the girl in your painting whom my husband was so enamoured of?'

'Was he now?' Barry Sothern cast a reflective look at Jason. 'I'd say your husband is a man very aware of his position and his possessions; he isn't the first of the type that I've encountered.'

'Really?' She raised her glass and sipped her wine, a fine rosé from the Devrel cellars. 'You intrigue me, Mr Sothern.'

'It's fascinating the way people run to types, and as an artist I'm very observant. This other man I mentioned, he had the same look of dangerous pride . . . rather like a tiger.'

'You speak like a writer.' Dinah was beginning to enjoy this conversation.

'Artists and writers have much in common,' he replied. 'We see things in rather more colourful ways than the normal run of people, and often we've struggled hard to gain success. Contrary to what everyone believes, we work hard at what we do, and though the end result might look as if it's been easily achieved, that is only an illusion. Nothing worthwhile comes without a struggle, whether it's career success or romantic happiness.'

'Do you love painting, Mr Sothern?' she asked.

'It's my life, Mrs Devrel.'

'Have you never married?'

He shook his head and suddenly his eyes were shadowed; those lion-like eyes were suddenly sombre. 'It was never my good fortune to be loved as I wanted to be loved. As you know, there are degrees of loving and some of us want the ultimate, as arrogant as it might sound. Some are fortunate and find what they need. I didn't, so I devoted myself to my work.'

'That sounds reasonable.' Dinah felt relaxed with this man, a tough but gentle giant, she told herself. 'I suppose my husband told you why he chose to consult you about my portrait?'

'He told me that he admired my work, which was gracious of him.'

'When Jason pays a compliment he means it, Mr Sothern. Jason rarely does or says anything that he doesn't mean, and it was at the Tate Gallery about a dozen years ago that he became spellbound by your painting of the girl Domini. I mentioned her a while ago—Jason told me she was beautiful and I wondered if you prefer to make portraits of beautiful girls.'

'I like to paint portraits of people with character,' he replied. 'Domini happened to be very beautiful, but she had something else that made her special, and had she been in an accident and become scarred I would still have—cared.'

'You cared very much, didn't you?' Dinah dared to say.

He nodded, and didn't speak again until their

second course was served, which was roast pork Caribbean style, with buttered French beans, potatoes boiled with chopped mint, and cauliflower whose flowerets were snowy white.

'This looks utterly delicious!' A smile had returned to the tanned and craggy face.

'Jason insists on the best, and that's why he wanted your talents.' Dinah returned his smile. 'You're very tanned, so I gather you've been working abroad—our weather is so unpredictable, isn't it?'

'Yes, it invariably rains when we want to watch cricket or play tennis or go to the Proms.' He sampled a mouthful of pork and his expression was a compliment to the chef. 'I actually live on the island of Crete, but every so often I spend time at my London studio. I happened to be there when your husband rang me and invited me to meet you.'

'Are you fond of the Greek isles?' Dinah asked, having no difficulty with her own appetite this evening.

'I've a great affection for Greece and the Greek people. They have great character, and once you gain their friendship, it's for life and totally loyal. You spoke of Domini whom I painted several times. She's the wife of a Greek, and rarely have I seen a couple so happy with each other. They're like the joined halves of a golden coin, you just can't imagine one without the other. Now and again I spend a holiday on Paul's island; he and Domini have a pair of fine children, but there was a time when she almost lost him to a dangerous

illness. I was selfish enough in those days to want
him out of the way, but now I realise that even if
Paul had died, Domini would never have turned
to another man. He had captured her body and
soul, and so I came to terms with the situation
and these days I have the friendship of both of
them. I value that friendship greatly.'

Barry Sothern glanced at Jason, studying him
in conversation with the doctor. It was as if the
artist couldn't quite make up his mind about
Jason, and Dinah wondered if he was comparing
her marriage to that of the girl he had loved.

'Jason has his values,' she said quietly, 'don't
make any mistake about that. He's a remarkably
generous man and he often fights with his fellow
board members over a loan they might feel isn't
backed by sufficient collateral. I happen to know
that he's supplied loans out of his private funds.'

'He was your guardian, wasn't he, Mrs Devrel?'

'Since I was nine years old.'

'A man might suspect that he has trained you
to be as he wants you,' he commented.

'And do you approve of his training?' asked
Dinah.

'In that dress you certainly do him credit, and
you speak up for his virtues like a dutiful wife.'

'I have to be a dutiful wife to Jason, because I
certainly can't be called a beautiful one, unlike
your friend's wife Domini.'

Immediately the sorrel eyes swept her face,
probing its contours, assessing its skin tone,
staying intent a moment upon the wide soft curve
of her lips.

'Beauty, Mrs Devrel, is in the eye of the beholder, as the old saying goes. Love can bring to life the plainest face.'

'Love?' she mocked. 'Isn't it the dream we never recall . . . the shadow beyond touch . . . the mystery of mysteries?'

'It can be tangible,' he said. 'You know when it becomes something you can touch.'

'Ah, but how quickly lost again.' Their eyes met and Dinah realised that she had told him in abstracts rather more than she had intended. He was *simpatico*, this man!

'Will you really paint me in this dress?' she asked, briskly changing the subject.

'Would you like to be painted in it?'

'I—don't know. This dress, Mr Sothern, has a tragic history.' Intentionally she raised her voice and sensed without looking that she had caught Jason's attention; the deep sound of his voice fell quiet and, feeling the drumming of her pulses, she went on: 'The woman it was intended for was killed in a car crash not so very far from Devrel Drive. Her car spun off the road, crashed down into the ravine and she was flung to her death.'

Silence filled the room, broken as Jason pushed back his chair and towered to his feet. 'Go and take that thing off!' His face was ashen with anger. 'How dare you even bring it into my house?'

His reaction was more dramatic than Dinah had anticipated, and her sense of triumph mingled with a certain dread. Only once before had she seen him look so furious, and making no attempt to control his temper he strode round the table to Dinah, and instinctively she cringed away from him.

He gripped hold of her chair, yanked it out from the table and jerked her to her feet. 'Go at once, or I shall haul you upstairs and tear the thing off your back!'

'Mr Devrel,' it was the doctor who spoke, 'I do beg of you not to unnerve your wife—I feel sure she meant no harm——'

'On the contrary, Dr Malcolm, she isn't a child who doesn't know wrong from right.' He spoke through his teeth, as if Dinah's action had set them on edge. 'Permit me to know Dinah as no other person in this world knows her—the little fool is paying me back because I won't let her drive her car!

'Well, isn't it so?' He pulled Dinah round to face him and shook her until her hair flopped into her eyes. 'You thought up this unamusing trick just to get at me, didn't you?'

'Yes, if you must know!' She met his enraged eyes with a defiant air. 'I had a feeling you wouldn't be amused.'

'I'll put you over my damned knee if you don't go upstairs and take the thing off!'

'Mr Sothern wants me to wear it for my portrait——'

'Over my dead body!' Still clasping her with his hands, Jason glanced at Barry Sothern, who was regarding the scene with narrowed eyes. 'I have the costume that I want Dinah to wear for her portrait; it belonged to my Spanish grandmother and it's been kept in excellent condition. It's a habit made especially for women who rode side-saddle, as was the fashion when she was a girl.'

His gaze came back to Dinah. 'Now, my graceless chit, you will march upstairs, take that dress off and replace it with something a little less macabre—do you hear me?'

'W-when you shout like that, Jason, I should imagine the dead can hear you!'

He gave her a none too gentle push towards the door, but instead of making her obedient to his command the push aroused her temper. 'I happen to like the dress,' she said stormily, 'and I don't happen to be riddled with superstition like you. I expect you get it from way back . . . the evil eye and all that!'

A jibe that really let loose the devils in Jason's eyes. 'Excuse us, will you?' he said to his guests, and the next moment Dinah was being forcibly marched from the room, across the hall and up the stairs. Jason's grip on her arm was like a vice, and much as she struggled she couldn't break free of him.

'Damned bully!' she stormed. 'You'll end up giving me a miscarriage!'

'Don't talk damned nonsense!' He marched her along the gallery. 'Dr Malcolm tells me that you're as vital as a young colt, and there are times when you're just as tiresome!'

'Because I won't tamely take the bit, Jason?'

He flung open the door of her bedroom and propelled her inside. 'Off with that rag, or shall I tear it off?'

'I'm sure it would give you a thrill to tear it off my back,' she rejoined. 'It seems to be part of your lovemaking technique!'

'Is that what you'd like, my sweet, some lovemaking?' He spun her around and began to pull at the back of the dress; the tiny hooks went all the way down to the bottom of her spine and there like a sheath it opened to release her. Jason lifted her out of the shadowed blue pool of silk, and suddenly she became aware of the gentling of his hands.

As he kicked the dress out of his way, Dinah turned to face him. Slowly she raised her arms and let them curl about his neck, like the small girl she used to be. 'You're fearfully angry with me, aren't you, Jason?'

'Don't you think I've reason to be?' He studied her face unsparingly, no softening in the lines of his mouth. 'I shall have to speak with Teri Lennox for allowing you to see the dress, let alone letting you buy it.'

'Don't blame Teri,' she pleaded. 'It was my idea—I wanted to—to——'

'I know what you wanted to do,' he said grimly. 'You take a perverse delight in making relations even more strained between us than they need to be. You want to smash to pieces what's left of our relationship, and you won't be satisfied until there's nothing left to patch up. Well, bear this in mind, Dinah, while you carry my child you'll behave in a reasonable manner. When you're delivered of the child you can go and sell Royal Doulton figurines in Timbuctoo for all I care!'

Her arms slid away from his shoulders as he straightened to his full height; she watched as he went across to the wardrobe where her dresses hung. He rattled the hangers and returned to her bedside with a girlish water-blue chiffon. 'Put this on—and don't take all night about it—and do something about your hair.'

'Yes, sir.'

For a moment more his face was imperious above her, his eyes like jet into which the lightly clad sight of her brought no warmth. 'We'll be taking coffee and cognac in the salon, so that's where you'll find us.'

The door closed behind him, and Dinah sank back on the bed in a reclining position, her gaze reflective. What, she wondered, was it like for those women who knew they were deeply loved and wanted; so that every inch of them was valued as well as desired? She rolled over on to her stomach, then remembered that she musn't do so and slid from the bed.

She walked over to the cheval mirror in its ornate frame and surveyed herself from head to toe. She raised a hand and removed her glasses, and instantly her reflection was softened and blurred so that she had to move nearer to the mirror in order to see her face more clearly.

Girls she had schooled with had been pretty, and some of them had seemed to pity her because she was so shortsighted and had to wear spectacles. She had been told more than once that men had the fixed idea that curvy vivacious girls with cute faces and bouncing hair were more fun to be with, and more likely to be responsive. Dinah had never pined for prettiness, but she was aware that girls who had it were far more popular in every way.

At the college dances her card had never overflowed with the names of young men clamouring to hold her close to them as the music played. Her weekends were spent studying, her nose in a book rather than pressed to a lean cheek while a young man stole a kiss or whispered compliments in her ear.

Jason was the only man who had ever paid serious attention to her, and the reason had been obvious to Teri Lennox, who had said that she had been trained to be his wife . . . the convenient wife for a man who was mainly interested in the family business, that of being a merchant banker. A man who in many ways preferred his home life to run on the smooth lines long since laid down by himself, and which a more demanding and egotistical wife might have disrupted. He had always known that Dinah wouldn't interfere with the smooth running of his household. She was friendly with the staff and wouldn't find new ways to upset their routine. She was a little cog in the machinery of his life who fitted in . . . she wasn't someone he passionately wanted just for herself.

Dinah turned from the mirror with a shrug and changed into the dress he had selected for her, and after tidying her hair as instructed she went downstairs and rejoined the party in the salon, where she sat down beside Dr Malcolm and quietly apologised for her behaviour.

'Put it down to the delicate condition I'm in,' she said, with a strained smile.

'As a matter of fact,' the doctor smiled, 'women do behave a trifle irrationally when they're pregnant, especially with a first child. It's caused by a dash of apprehension mixed with resentment because they aren't going to be thought of as young girls any more. Being a mother is quite a responsibility. In lots of ways it's an honour.'

'An honour?' Dinah echoed, accepting cognac in her coffee and stirring it in with a little golden spoon that matched the rims of the delicate cups. They were Chinese, like the salon itself, with its exotic furniture, amazingly lovely carpets and walls hung with paintings on silk.

'Think about it, Dinah,' the doctor urged. 'Haven't you realised that a miracle is going on inside your body? A human being is forming there and, God willing, that being will have a brain, plump little limbs to wave about in the air, eyes that smile at you, and arms that reach out to you. I repeat, my dear, it's a great honour to be a mother.'

'I agree with your philosophy, Dr Malcolm.' Barry Sothern had strolled over quietly and overheard. 'Most of nature is mysterious and wonderful if you take the time to study it. From tiny seeds grow giant trees, and from an embrace a child is born. It takes my breath away, and I'm something of a hardened sinner!'

'We all commit sins, Mr Sothern, but in our way we make up for them.' Dr Malcolm spoke with a quiet, sincere wisdom, learned in her trade. 'Each one of us is a divided creature; like the moon we have a dark side, and there are impulses inside us that sway us between good and bad. We are very much a part of nature and we have our stormy nights and our halcyon days.'

An hour slipped away while they talked. Dinah didn't say much and was content to listen to these people who were older than she and more experienced. Then Dr Malcolm had to make her departure in order to visit a patient; she had her car with her and she assured Jason that she was a careful driver and didn't need to be escorted home.

Jason walked with her to her car, and after a moment Dinah said to Barry Sothern: 'Have you changed your mind about painting me now you've found out that I can be mean to Jason?'

'I want to paint your portrait very much,' he reassured her. 'Believe me, I understand what you're going through.'

'You can't know,' she protested. 'We've only just met!'

'I sense that Jason Devrel has married you without giving you the chance to savour the world of other men.'

Dinah gazed at him wide-eyed. 'Is that what happened to the girl you loved?'

'Not exactly, but I'm right about you, aren't I?'

Dinah traced with a fingertip the embroidered dragon on the cushion where she reclined. 'Is Domini very beautiful, Mr Sothern?'

'A lot of it comes from within . . . like you, she has fire burning under the water-cool look.'

Dinah caught her breath. 'No—I'm very placid.'

He shook his head and his eyes crinkled; in their depths lay his observant knowledge of people. 'You're too young as yet to really know yourself . . . you never were precocious, were you?'

'Jason wouldn't approve of a pert child who poked her nose in his business or his cupboards.' She tried to speak lightly, but the artist had startled her with his observation about her inner self . . . his intimation that she might be passionate without being fully awake to her own nature. It was an intriguing idea . . . also it was a little alarming.

'Are you going to accept Jason's suggestion that you portray me in the riding habit his Spanish grandmother used to wear?'

Barry Sothern gave a slight laugh. 'I don't really know what to say, except that it will depend on the garment itself. I don't want you to look anything but yourself——'

'Glasses and all?' she interjected.

He leaned forward and gently took the spectacles off her nose; then he quietly studied her face. 'You need to wear these, of course?'

She nodded. 'I'm myopic. I can see things at a distance only if I wear my specs, and when I take them off even close things become rather blurred.'

'There's an operation these days that can correct it, you know. Has your husband never made enquiries? He strikes me as a man who is very much in the know.'

'Jason,' she shrugged, 'isn't bothered by my glasses and I'm used to wearing them. Let's face it, Mr Sothern, I wouldn't be any use as a contestant for the Miss Havenshore beauty contest even if my short sight could be corrected.'

'So you aren't vain?'

'We-ell, I like nice clothes and I—I don't think my figure's too bad.' Then she gave a laugh. 'Not at the present time, but it won't be too long before I lose my sylph-like figure—do you take long to paint a portrait?'

'Depends on the subject. A side-saddle riding habit reminds me of Edwardian days, and you haven't quite that look I've seen in the faces of women of that era—disdain and a certain narrowness of mind.'

'Jason's grandmother didn't come out of the Ark,' Dinah protested with a touch of indignation. 'She was a woman with a very definite style and she dressed to suit herself. Jason resembles her physically and they were very compatible; he used to go and stay with her in Spain when he was young. You should paint him in a suit of lights; he has one, which was given to him by Ruy de Mendos only a short while before he was killed in the Madrid arena. Jason admires the courage of the matadors, but he despises the bullfight itself.'

'I can see that he'd look the part,' Barry Sothern reflected. 'Do you think he'd object if I called you Dinah? You're so young and I'm old enough to be your father——' The artist broke off, as if realising that Jason could be her father as well, had he been precocious as a teenager.

'I'd like you to ask his permission,' Dinah said demurely. 'I don't mind you calling me by my first name, but he might—he's an unpredictable man.'

'So you're obedient to his wishes ninety per cent of the time, then you break out and really get him stirred up?'

'You mean that business with the dress?'

'I thought he was going to put you over his knee right in front of the doctor and myself!' A smile clefted Barry Sothern's cheek. 'You knew his reaction would be dramatic, didn't you?'

'Yes,' she admitted. 'He was at the scene of the accident and because of it he thinks I'll go and drive myself over the edge of the ravine. He's so terribly possessive ... sometimes I catch him looking at me with those hawkish eyes of his as if he wants to get into my mind as well as my body——' She broke off, biting her lip as Jason strolled into the salon. Had he heard her remark? His ears were as quick as his eyes and though he looked impertubable, she was aware of how swiftly he could mask his feelings.

'Aren't you smoking, Mr Sothern?' He flung open the lid of a carved humidor and offered the artist one of his imported cigars, long, slim, in a wrapper of rustling leaf.

In a while the salon was redolent of aromatic cigar smoke, which didn't upset Dinah at all. It was familiar as the scent of roses in the bowls on low lacquered tables. Familiar as the Tang dragon in an alcove, a green and shining fantasy of fierceness.

'I was wondering——?'

'Yes, Mr Sothern?' From the depths of his chair Jason regarded the other man with slightly hooded eyes.

'As I shall be coming regularly to your house for the portrait sittings, may I call both of you by your first names? It makes things less formal.'

'By all means.' Smoke wreathed into the air from Jason's cigar. 'Tell me, what do you think of my suggestion that Dinah be costumed in the riding habit that was my grandmother's? My wife does ride, so she won't look awkward in it.'

'I would like to see the outfit before I decide.'

'I anticipated that you would.' Jason rose from his chair and went across to one of the lacquered cabinets, from which he took a large square box. 'I brought this down earlier today; I'd already decided that if you agreed to paint Dinah's portrait I'd want her to wear this for the sittings.'

Clenching his cigar in his teeth, Jason lifted the lid from the box and withdrew the riding habit from its wrapping of thin silk in which it had reposed ever since he had brought it back to England along with other mementoes of his holidays in Spain. He shook the long skirt and jacket and displayed them, deep violet-coloured cashmere cut with precision and perfect Andalucian detail.

'What a superb colour!' Barry Sothern leapt to his feet and went across to examine the riding habit more closely. 'Yes, you're absolutely right about this, Jason. It's feminine and boyish at the same time and your wife will look—vulnerable, I think, a look I want to bring out. It's a colour that will set off her skin.'

Jason gave him a quick look, his eyes impenetrable jet in his dark face. 'You're very observant, aren't you?' he drawled, his eyes settling on Dinah as he resumed his seat and left the artist to hold the habit to the light so he could absorb a colour that was rich without being garish.

'Aren't you clever, Jason?' Dinah sat hugging one of the dragon-embroidered cushions. 'You always get your way, don't you?'

'I get my way if it happens to be right.' He drew on his cigar and released the smoke from his nostrils. 'Even had that dress been unconnected with a tragic accident I should still have wanted you to wear the riding habit. Not only from sentimental reasons but because, as Barry remarked, it will show off your skin.'

'Won't my glasses detract from the effect?' she murmured.

'You won't need to wear them for the sittings.' Barry carefully replaced the habit in its box and closed the lid. 'It won't matter if you can only see my battered face through a mist. It will be a blessing in disguise.'

'I think you have a very interesting face—Barry.' Dinah gave him the smile which she denied Jason, with his annoying ability to run her life even when she attempted to oppose him.

'You have a kind heart, Dinah.' Barry stood puffing on his cigar, his eyes smouldering with the fires of creative energy. 'I can't wait to get started on your portrait—I realise, Jason, that Dinah is pregnant, so what do you say to two-hour sittings each morning from ten o'clock to noon?'

'What do you think, Dinah?' Jason quirked an enquiring brow. 'Will two hours tire you?'

'Of course not! I'm not an invalid, you know.'

'Will Dinah be seated?' asked Jason.

'I can't quite decide.' Barry blew a swirl of cigar smoke. 'The riding habit is so striking that I think it would be a pity not to show it on Dinah in a standing position. I would certainly ensure that she takes three or four rests during the posings.'

'I'll be perfectly all right, Jason.' Dinah gave an airy laugh. 'You worry more about my state of pending motherhood than I do! And I fully agree with Barry's suggestion; the habit will look bulky if I sit in it, and the skirt should flow. I'll let him know soon enough if I start getting the vapours.'

'Very well, the matter's decided.' Jason looked at Barry. 'When do you want to begin the sittings?'

'Tuesday morning, if I may? I shall need Monday in order to make my preparations.'

'And how long do you usually take to complete a painting?'

'It varies. Sometimes I start and then I'm not satisfied with the pose or the position of the light, but in general I take about three weeks.'

'Sounds fine to me. Shall we drink on it?'

'That certainly sounds like a good idea.'

Jason drew the cork of a bottle of vintage Bollinger and when he handed Dinah her glass of the sparkling champagne she met his eyes and remembered their wedding reception ... would she ever belong to herself and not be owned and directed by a man who didn't even love her?

The three of them clinked glasses to the success of the portrait.

'Does the idea excite you, Dinah?' Barry smiled down at her.

'Yes,' she admitted, 'but I have the feeling I shall be the peahen in your gallery of beauties. Perhaps you should paint Jason instead of me?'

'Dressed in your plumage you won't know yourself.' Barry spoke confidently. 'It isn't every skin that can take such a shade of violet, rather like those shadows seen in the sky in midsummer, when the afterglow fades and night falls softly.'

When he spoke those words Dinah thought that his voice had a Welsh intonation, like a certain famous actor whose films she enjoyed.

'All right,' she said, 'I place myself in your hands, Barry, and Jason can add one more Devrel bride to those who already adorn the walls of this house. Have you seen the portrait of his Spanish grandmother?'

'I'd very much like to,' Barry said at once, and the three of them walked out of the salon and crossed the hall to where the large, gold-framed portrait hung against the oak panelling. Doña Manuela, who had handed on to Jason the dark Latin eyes with such depths to them, the proud and haughty features, and the raven hair.

'How can I compete?' asked Dinah, with a wry smile. 'Isn't she splendid?'

Barry's observant gaze dwelt upon the hand holding a black lace fan, seeing there the same ring that adorned Dinah's hand. 'May I?' he took hold of Dinah's left hand and studied the ring. 'I must make sure to include this in your portrait; a fascinating link between the generations, so that as your child grows up you can point out to him or her the lovely family heirloom.'

'But I shan't——' Dinah broke off and withdrew her hand from Barry's. 'Jason is the one who believes in carrying on family traditions, so he'll have to do as you suggest.'

Something in her voice must have told Barry that emotions between her and Jason were charged with a force that wasn't a happy one, and he took a quick look at his wristwatch and said it was about time for him to bid them au revoir until Tuesday morning. He had rented a cottage in the nearby village of Penlyn, so he could commute easily to the house on Devrel Drive.

'It's been a most enjoyable evening,' he said warmly, and while Jason was seeing him off, out there on the steps where the hall lights spilled and framed their tall figures, Dinah ran up the stairs and went to her suite.

She had told Hester not to wait up for her, and as she closed the door she deliberately slid the brass bolt, pushing it firmly into position. Then she undressed, took a warm shower and slowly towelled herself. She had enjoyed the evening as well and was quite taken with the idea of being painted by a man as interesting as Barry Sothern.

It would assist some of the time in passing,

shorten those endless weeks while she waited for
Jason's baby to be born. She slid a hand over her
body, feeling the curve where the child was
growing. She was apprehensive, as Dr Malcolm
had guessed, and there was more than a dash of
resentment in her heart. A child should be made
with love and tender desire, not be the outcome
of a battle of wills.

In his strength and determination Jason had
won that battle ... her resistance had been
overcome and his possession of her had been
total, so that never would she forget those hours
in his arms, when the touch of his hands had
quickened her unwilling senses to such a pitch of
sensual need that nothing on earth could stop the
assuagement that took place.

The memory of it all was as certain in Dinah's
mind as the child she carried in her body, and
hastily she slid a silky sleeveless nightdress down
over her body where traitorous urges were at her
nerve ends when she allowed herself to think of
Hallowe'en night.

She was reading a magazine in bed when she
heard the handle of her door being tried. She
watched with a kind of fascination as the handle
turned left and right ... left and right. Instinct
told her it was Jason, but he couldn't get in,
because the bolt was a strong one and it was only
in films that impassioned men broke into a
woman's bedroom by using brute force. Jason
wouldn't attempt such a foolish action, for he
knew how solid were the oak doors of his house.

Dinah envisioned him in his sombre well-cut

robe, looking almost monk-like as he stood there, dark eyes hooded in thought. Instinct had warned her that he would come to her room tonight. He had been terribly angered by that scene with the dress . . . but during their struggle, while he had ripped it from her body, she had felt a kind of excitement between them, smouldering, wanting to leap free of the constraints they put upon themselves.

Dinah slid down in her bed, listening to the silence broken softly by the ticking of her bedside clock . . . her limbs felt hot and languid within the confines of her nightdress, it seemed to stifle her and she wanted to be free of it.

Total silence seemed to seep in from the gallery, and she turned her cheek into her pillow and was reaching to the lamp switch when the doors of her balcony were pushed open and Jason came in out of the night. For shocked seconds Dinah couldn't move, then she sat up and confronted him. 'W-what do you want?' Her eyes were huge, trying to see him clearly as he came towards her bed.

'Tonight, my dear, I've decided that I want you,' he replied, and as he spoke he began to remove his robe.

'G-go away——' Dinah pulled the sheet up against herself. 'You haven't any right to come in here—we came to an arrangement and you promised——'

'This wouldn't be happening, Dinah, if you hadn't bolted your door against me.' He loomed over her, his torso strong and tawny above her cowering figure. 'I merely meant to look in so we could have a few words about the portrait, but bolting that door combined with wearing that infernal dress has tried my patience beyond the limit!'

His hand jerked the sheet away and his eyes raked over her body in the pale silk, a slim strap fallen from her shoulder to expose the delicate contour. His fingers stroked her skin and explored the slim column of her neck before moving down over her softness; all the way down to where her stomach curved.

Dinah heard him catch his breath and she knew what he was thinking . . . this was his baby and she was his because of what had transpired to make that burgeoning life inside her.

'So sweetly amazing,' he breathed. 'I heard what the doctor said to you, and I have to agree with her.'

'That it's an honour?' Dinah was trying her best to push him away from her, but he was so strong, so persistent, so much closer all the time. 'An honour to be—like this?'

'You excite me—like this.' He cradled her up against him and ran his lips over her face. 'Don't fight me, Dinah . . . don't fight me this time.'

Dinah could feel a dangerous languor creeping over her . . . her body wanted what Jason was doing even as her mind strove to remind her that this was a man she must distrust. Submission was only a sign to him that he was having his own way again.

'Stop it—go away!' She pummelled his chest

and shoulders, but it was like hitting warm smooth iron; her blows had far less effect on him than his kisses and stroking had on her.

'Damn you!' she whimpered, and he laughed softly as he closed each of her eyes with his marauding lips. Her senses swam as he stroked his hand across her hips and breasts; she quivered beneath his wandering hand, felt a languorous aching as he breathed into her ear that she felt like silk . . . hot sweet silk.

There was no time, past or present, and nothing began to matter except that the fires of feeling leapt through flesh and bone. Her arms clung about his neck and the great wide pupils of her eyes were filled with his image there above her, his black hair in disarray upon his brow, his dark eyes ablaze with the fire he generated between them, stoking it until it soared, white-hot and wonderful.

It was she who cried out, and then her hands travelled up and down his back, feeling the movements of his muscles beneath the moist skin, hearing his deep intakes of breath.

She lay clasped to him as if the scorching pleasure had welded them limb to limb. Something molten and moving flowed all through her . . . it felt . . . it felt like joy.

Jason lay tense as she lay silent, and then he drew away from her and slid from the bed, reaching for the robe that clad him again in dark aloofness . . . an intimate stranger walking away towards the balcony windows through which he had entered.

'Goodnight, Dinah,' he flung over his shoulder. 'Sweet dreams.'

He closed the windows behind him and was gone, leaving Dinah to pull the covers around herself. The molten joy went cold inside her and she lay there feeling as if used . . . Jason had used her without love and left her with the careless arrogance of a man who merely owned her.

Her hurt was too deep for anger. She felt that she wanted never to see his face again, because to look in his eyes would be to see herself abandoned to him, lost to the sensations he made her feel without feeling a spark of love for her.

Suddenly she couldn't stand the thoughts and feelings he had left her with, and leaping from the disordered bed she ran into the bathroom and stood beneath the pounding shower for minutes on end.

At last, wearing her towelling robe, she dried her hair with the hand dryer and welcomed the warm flow of air through her hair; it was so soothing, easing away the weak need to weep. Finally tiredness came to her rescue and she fell asleep on the daybed, wrapped in a spare blanket. Nothing could have induced her to return to the big bed, to spend the night remembering.

The dream that followed her through the night was of the sea pounding on to rocks . . . pounding them to drifts of sand that blew through the hollows of a dark cavern.

CHAPTER EIGHT

IT certainly was no chore for Dinah having her portrait put on canvas, for at the end of each half hour Barry permitted her to relax.

Coffee and doughtnuts would be served to them, and he warned her on the day he started to paint her that she wasn't going to be allowed to see her portrait until it was completed and he was fully satisfied with it. And each day when he left the house the painting was covered by American cloth which had leather straps he actually locked, ensuring the secrecy of his work until he was ready to reveal it.

'Don't you trust me?' Dinah wanted to know.

'Women are notoriously inquisitive,' he retorted. 'And at this stage of the portrait you might not like what you see and it might change the look in your eyes.'

'And what look is that?' she asked. 'Don't all shortsighted people look as if they're peering through a mist?'

'In a way,' he agreed, 'and it adds a certain vulnerability, because they're aware that there are things to stumble over and they don't go striding all over other people.'

'Is that how you think of Jason?' Her husband was a subject Barry was inclined to avoid, as if he hadn't yet decided whether he liked the man she was married to.

'Jason Devrel knows his place in life,' said Barry, a single bite of his firm teeth halving a jam doughnut. 'If there is anything he's unsure of, he conceals it well.'

'Don't you care for him?' Dinah wanted to know. 'I've noticed that most mornings you manage to arrive just as he's left for the bank.'

'I have my reason,' Barry finished his coffee. 'Ready to take up your position again?'

'In a minute, Barry. Tell me first what that reason is.'

'You see, I said all women are inquisitive.'

'Please tell me!' she begged.

'He's a demanding man, Dinah. He would ask to see what I've so far accomplished of your portrait, and I don't intend to show him.'

'Nervous of him?' she taunted.

'Not of him, but of his reaction. I might——' Barry hesitated, 'I might be unveiling for others what he considers to be his and only his, if that doesn't sound too complex.'

She considered his words. 'It isn't complex—I know what you mean.'

'Do you, Dinah?'

'Yes.' She flushed at a recent memory of herself in Jason's arms. 'Jason doesn't love me, but I—I evoke desire in him. He's possessive of me, not because I'm pretty or seductive. I am for Jason, and always will be, the little girl lost who came into his house eleven years ago. Oh, how tall he seemed to me! He leaned down and picked me up in his arms and I started to cry. I felt so lost, so lonely, because I knew I'd never see my parents again. Jason carried me into the music room and put me down in one of the big leather chairs, then he went to the piano and started to play some Chopin. I suppose I knew, even then, that he'd decided to own me . . . that he'd kill me rather than let me get away from him!'

'My dear Dinah——'

'But I did get away from him for a while,' she confided. 'It didn't last, of course. He came looking for me and he found me, and there was nothing else I could do but marry him.'

The mornings in Barry's company passed pleasantly, but they never talked of her marriage again. Barry understood that she had said more than she had intended, but his attitude of kindness towards her had intensified. He had become a friend and she was grateful for his company.

One morning she said to him: 'Did you ever paint Domini to your complete satisfaction?'

He shook his head. 'I was in love with her, and for a man in love the woman is forever changing. For me, painting Domini was rather like the great Turner forever painting his seascapes. It's the changeability of people rather than the constancy that makes them appealing—at least, I believe so.'

'And you found Domini very appealing, didn't you, Barry?'

'Constantly appealing,' he smiled, a man come to terms with the pain of unrequited love. 'I never expected to find again that kind of appeal.'

His gaze dwelt upon Dinah for several seconds, then he leaned forward to add a stroke of the brush to the portion of her face or figure that he was painting as they conversed.

'You're very appealing, Dinah, and just like Domini you don't fully realise it, and you certainly don't use it for your own ends. Unaware women are a rarity—and I speak from experience; I've painted a considerable number of women in my time, and those with the deep inner self have always been the most interesting to put on canvas, whether plain or pretty. An artist can sometimes reveal in their expression what they conceal.'

'And you are doing that where I'm concerned.' She smiled but felt at the same time a little flurry of alarm inside her. Was she going to like this portrait when she eventually saw it? But more important, was Jason going to approve?

'Don't get impatient,' Barry grinned. 'The day will come when I'll permit you to look at yourself.'

'And what if I dislike myself?'

'I shall be desolated.'

'What if Jason doesn't like what he sees?'

'I expect he'll pay my exorbitant fee and put the portrait in one of his attics, but in the meantime, young woman, take that look off your face!'

'What look?'

'You're turning down your lip because in your heart you want your husband to think I've made you beautiful?'

'And have you?' Her breath caught on a laugh. 'No, you're too honest a painter for that, aren't you?'

'Ridiculously honest. Beauty is skin-deep ... it's mystery that makes a woman.'

'I have mystery, Barry?' Dinah was intrigued by the idea.

'You are like a seashell, both delicate and deep,' he told her.

'H'm, I hope this isn't going to be one of those abstract paintings, with me as a pregnant seashell on a beach with the tide coming in?'

He gave a throaty laugh. 'Do you think your husband would find such an abstraction to his taste?'

'So basically it's Jason who has to be gratified?'

'I hope you'll both be gratified.' Barry gave her a quizzical look. 'Do you know, Dinah, if women ever succeed in their unisex aims, then they're going to be the most dissatisfied creatures who ever walked this earth. Men and women are two separate species; they neither think alike nor look alike, and the exciting thing about a male and a female is that they are different. Not unequal in any sense of the word, but as different from each other as night and day.'

'And which is night?' she asked.

'Do you really need to ask?'

'Women are the night creatures, is that what you're saying?'

'Inevitably. They've more bodily secrets than men, and most of those secrets are connected with making love.'

'And love is made at night,' she murmured.

'That really is the best time for it,' he smiled. 'The night holds mystery, it's elemental and arouses the imagination. Also at that time most of us are in the warm, intimate cosiness of the bed.'

'This conversation is getting a little *risqué*!' she exclaimed. 'Suppose my husband was to walk in and hear us talking of love?'

'Are you afraid he'd break my neck?'

'He'd probably break mine first!'

'I don't doubt that he's an infernally jealous fellow, but I can't believe, Dinah, that he'd damage any portion of your body.'

'Because of the baby?'

'No, not because you're carrying his child. Do you want me to tell you what he said when I asked him why he wanted me to paint you?'

'I—I'm sure it had something to do with the Devrel tradition—the wives are always painted.'

'That's only part of it, Dinah. He paid me the compliment of saying that I was the artist who was best at capturing the essence of a person. He said he didn't want a chocolate-box picture of you; he wanted the truth of you—the elusive truth.'

'I see. And that is what you're painting?'

Barry inclined his head. 'I'm attempting it, and I can but hope that he accepts my portrayal of you. There is a sadness deep in your eyes, my dear child. I can't put happiness there if it isn't there. He must accept that.'

'Don't worry,' she said. 'Jason knows I'm not all sweetness and light because he made a Devrel of me. He knows I'm like a wren in a cage, pining to be free of it. He—he made me marry him!'

'Like Domini,' Barry murmured. 'Just like

Domini, who believed Paul only wanted her body.'

'Don't most men want that?' Dinah spoke with sudden coldness. 'Do men really care about our feelings?'

'Some do, Dinah. Some don't. It's all in the game.'

'Game?' she echoed. 'I like the word you use!'

'That's how life is played, Dinah. Sometimes we win a point, sometimes we lose one. I'm a lot older than you, so I'm a wiser participant, and make no mistake about it, men need love as much as women. You've heard that song from *South Pacific*, haven't you? There isn't anything like a dame, and men who drill for oil, who go and fight the battles and step out into space to explore, they can't wait to get romantic with a girl.'

'It's obvious you're a romantic, Barry!' she smiled.

'I'd be a lousy artist if I wasn't. Most of the arts are centred on romance; take those Fred Astaire movies you tell me you enjoy.'

Her eyes softened and she heaved a little sigh. 'Those tunes, those words, those two people making love to dance time. You've almost convinced me, Barry.'

'Almost?' he quizzed. 'You're standing out against a complete surrender?'

'There was a time——' She gave a slight shrug, then remembered that she must maintain the pose which had been Barry's idea. She stood at the foot of the staircase, with its wide treads and carved oak framing her figure in the violet-

coloured habit which had needed very little
alteration in order to fit her. Doña Manuela had
not been a large woman, and Dinah felt quite at
ease in the riding clothes and had been shown by
Barry how to drape the skirt so her riding boots
added that dash of boyishness he wanted.

Because she leaned slightly against the balus-
trade the pose wasn't a tiring one, and though she
was by no means a vain girl she was pleased that
for her portrait she wouldn't be an Orphan Annie
in glasses. Normally she had to wear the darn
things, but they were so unglamorous, and in her
secret heart she wanted her son or daughter to
look at her in her picture frame and not be too
disappointed.

'Dinah?'

'Sorry, did I move?'

'No, my dear, but I was just wondering what it
is that troubles you so—can't you tell me?'

She shook her head.

'I'm good at listening,' Barry told her.

'I know you are, but——'

'There are some things not for telling, eh?'

'Tell me about Crete. Talk me out of the blues,
Barry.'

He obligingly did so, and in the days that
followed Dinah learned quite a lot of pleasant
things about Greece, where he had a villa and
where the light for painting was the best he'd
ever come across. He talked about his Greek
friends, and Dinah thought what a waste it was
that this big, wise, talented man didn't have a
wife and family.

He seemed to believe in love, while she was afraid to do so. How could she tell him what it was like to live with a man like Jason? She was Jason's possession; when he looked at her, when he touched her, it was with ownership.

Love was something you gave, not something you took. That was how she knew that Jason didn't love her ... she was merely his, like the items of jade and amber he would lift from a table to fondle for a while, then he would replace the item and walk away to some desk work. Always his desk in the den was a battlefield of documents and thick folders, and Masefield, his secretary, was like a gnome in there, rarely emerging because there were always letters to answer and figures to be checked.

As a little girl in this large house Dinah used to think that Masefield lived on mushrooms, because he so reminded her of a garden gnome with his grizzled hair and his wise, abstracted face. Later on she learned that he really lived on chicken sandwiches and coffee, and was addicted to a briar pipe he would smoke in the garden when he took a break.

She had long since realised that when people came to work for Jason they rarely left the job; the staff had a tendency to intermarry, and her young maid Hester was in a glow because the chauffeur had recently put a pearl ring upon her left hand.

There were times when Dinah envied Hester that light in her brown eyes, that lightness of step of a girl walking on air because she knew herself loved.

One evening at the mirror while Hester stood brushing Dinah's hair they discussed the girl's forthcoming marriage, which was being conducted in the ancient little church in the village where Hester had grown up and gone to school.

'I couldn't think of being married in anything but white, Miss Dinah.' She drew the brush slowly down the long smooth hair. 'My dad's paying for my dress, and my gran is lending the veil that she wore at her wedding. It's yards long and was brought home from Brussels by Gran's older brother who was with the ambulances in that horrible war. It's sort of ivory-coloured with age but ever so lovely, and they say something old brings luck, don't they?'

Dinah studied the girl's glowing face through the mirror and remembered her own wedding day. 'I don't think you'll need too much luck, Hester. I'm sure Jenkins is the soul of kindness to you.'

'He is, Miss Dinah, even though my ma says he's a bit on the mature side for me. But as I told her, Mr Jason is an older man, and look at the care he takes of you!'

'My husband,' Dinah smiled wryly, 'takes good care of all his possessions. Has he asked you yet what you want for a wedding present?'

Hester nodded shyly. 'I told him I'd love one of those new fridge-freezers on the market, and he's going to order it so it can be delivered to the cottage while Jeff and me are on our honeymoon.' A blush swept over Hester's face, increasing the natural country rosiness of her skin. 'We're going to Wales, Miss Dinah. Jeff has relatives in Cymru and Jeff tells me it's ever so lovely there.'

'You're a lucky girl, Hester.' Dinah spoke from her heart. 'I want to give you a present as well, something more personal than a fridge-freezer. I'll arrange for my dressmaker to see you and measure you for a negligee and nightdress for your honeymoon; would you like that?'

'My Jeff will,' Hester said delightedly. 'You are kind and thoughtful, Miss Dinah.'

'Oh, it's easy to be kind to nice people, Hester, and you're such a pretty girl that you should have something as stunning to wear on your wedding night as the white dress you'll wear in the church.'

'I bet you wanted to wear white, didn't you, Miss Dinah?'

'It would have been nice.' As Dinah rose from the dressing stool she pressed a hand against herself, for she had begun to notice the slight weight of the child whenever she stood up. It had grown from an abstract, guilty secret into a tiny human being who was her constant companion. When she let herself think about that little curled-up creature she felt such a pull on her heartstrings that she wanted to cry out with the pain.

When the time came for her to hear her baby's first cry, how could she bring herself to leave?

Jason . . . Jason had known how she would feel . . . he had banked on it happening to her, this love of his child spreading through the very marrow of her bones and binding her to the baby long before its birth.

'Are you feeling all right, Miss Dinah?' The concern in Hester's voice recalled her from her thoughts.

'Yes,' she smiled, 'I'm fine. I'll go to bed now and have a read of that baby book that Jason had sent down from Hatchard's.'

She did read for a while, then turned out the lamp and lay in the dark listening to the sea pounding the rocks far below the house. The sound rose upwards because the house was built into the cliffs, its foundations of the same granite. There were caves that extended right beneath those foundations, so that when the tides rushed in they brought their echoes with them.

It was a sound that had followed Dinah into sleep from her first night in Jason's house. When she was away at school and college she missed that nocturnal lullaby of the elements and she would be restless at night for a while.

It had been like that in London at the hostel. She had to listen to passing traffic instead of the rolling waves and the splash of water as the waves hit the rocks, moving closer all the time until they pounded the cliffside.

Then early in the morning the seabirds would mew and squall and cling to the ledges of cliff stone, rising up on black and white wings to strut upon the balconies of the house.

Dinah finally fell asleep, to awake with a start some time later. She sat up with a startled, rather creepy feeling that made her peer through the darkness as if she sensed a lurking presence. She gave a shiver as coldness brushed the bare skin of

her arms ... the curtains were open and
billowing slightly, but it wasn't from the
direction of the windows that she had felt that
eerie, unearthly movement.

'Jason—is that you?'

There was no reply, and Dinah told herself not
to be absurd. He couldn't come silently through
an oaken door; she was such a light sleeper that
she always awoke if Hester or the housekeeper
looked in on her ... she knew they'd been given
orders to do so in case she took it into her head to
run away again.

Right now she felt like running from this room,
so large, so filled with shadows in its far corners
... quickly she slid down in the big bed and
pulled the covers up to her face, hiding like a
schoolgirl from imagined terrors.

Then gradually her nerves took control of her
thoughts and she couldn't stop herself from
thinking of the film she had watched the other
evening while Jason was out on business. The
story had been that of a young baby-minder alone
with two young children; alone downstairs while
they slept, with a telephone that rang every few
minutes, the voice on the line whispering and
threatening. Though she was unnerved by the
film the acting had absorbed Dinah until the end,
when Jason had walked into the music room to
find her huddled in one of the big chairs,
clutching a cushion to her, still shaken by the
horrific finale.

Jason had ordered her not to watch late-night
movies again, then as in the old days he had

carried her upstairs . . . she had thought he was
heading for his bedroom, but he had brought her
to her own and left her with a polite goodnight
and a reiteration that films about baby-minders
in lonely houses were off her agenda until their
own baby was born.

Suddenly Dinah could stand no more of her
thoughts. She scrambled out of bed, snatched her
robe, thrust her feet into her slippers and ran to
the door. Her hand fumbled with the handle,
then she was out on the silent gallery with its dim
lights and running among the shadows in the
direction of Jason's bedroom.

Instinct drove her there, she wanted to be safe
from her fears . . . from the phantoms, real or
imaginary, that chose to walk through her mind
tonight.

She found his door and as she opened it the
sound must have disturbed Jason's sleep at once.
'Who is that?' he muttered.

'It's me——' Now she was actually here Dinah
felt subdued, blinking in the sudden dazzle of
light as he switched on his bedside lamp.

'Are you not feeling well?' he demanded, his
hair sleep-ruffled as he stared across the room at
her hesitant figure in the doorway.

'I——' She took a tentative step towards him.
'I was suddenly afraid—I thought there was
someone in my room——'

'You've been having a nightmare, probably
brought on by all those biscuits and that wedge of
cheese.'

'Yes, I suppose it was the cheese.' She edged

forward, for in the rays of the lamp he looked so big and solid, while out there on the gallery a figure in grey draperies might be watching for her. 'Can I—stay with you?'

He didn't answer right away, and because she couldn't quite make out the expression on his face she assumed rejection and took a step backwards.

'All right, I'll go——'

'Come here, you little fool!'

Dinah flung the door shut and ran to him, flinging herself down beside him and pressing her head to his shoulder. His hand stroked her hair, feeling large and warm as it enclosed her skull. 'You had pickles as well, as I recall.'

She nodded.

'Come then, in you get.' He opened the covers for her, and she didn't miss the catch of his breath as she dropped her robe and he saw her in her lacy nightdress. As she slid into the warm bed with him, he turned out the lamp and drew her into his arms. As they closed firm and strong around her, Dinah breathed his skin and hair and warm breath.

'Am I shutting out the terrors?' he murmured. 'Are they going away, my strange and troubled Dinah?'

'You must think me very childish——'

'I just think you very pregnant and a little too fond of mixed pickles.' As he spoke he fondled her, and very gently touched his mouth to hers. 'I'll do a thorough job of driving away the hobgoblins if you like?'

Dinah lay there in the security of his arms and let herself drift into the sensuality of his closeness and his touch. He seemed so very human right now, his the body which had made her baby, that small bundle of mixed genes and impulses shared with him. She took his hand and pressed it to the swell of her, feeling his hard long legs enwrapping hers until all at once she was one with him, locked together by a desire that again flowed hot and sweet through every cell of her body.

She could hear herself crying out his name as she clung helplessly to his smooth, moist shoulders, then she lay in the fold of his arms and a rosy flush engulfed her. Thrills of afterglow ran over her skin and she gave a satisfied sigh that stirred the hair of his chest.

'That sent the hobgoblins back where they came from, wouldn't you say so, Dinah?' He moved his lips on the silky skin of her neck. 'It's a real pleasure when you give yourself.'

'Did I do that, Jason?'

'Very conclusively!'

She gazed into his eyes as if trying to discover what lay at the very depths of their darkness. Right now they were slumbrous, and she wondered if her baby would have such thick, black lashes.

'There are times when you're really quite sensitive, Jason,' she murmured.

'Did you think, my dear, that I was made of leather?'

'The parts of you that show are rather leathery.' She traced his features with a fingertip, down through the groove in his cheek to the edge of his mouth. He took her finger into his mouth and she felt herself getting excited by him again.

'Oh—Jason,' she whispered suddenly.

'God, this is sweet!' He crushed her lips with his and her senses reeled as he took her ... took her far out where the stars pulsed and tumbled through a sensational void.

While he slept she lay wide-eyed in the darkness, listening to him as he breathed at her side, his dark head resting against her. How strange their relationship was, so that sometimes it felt so right, and at other times felt so wrong. Why was it that when she found herself in his arms she wanted him, yet when she was out of them she rebelled and thought of herself as a prisoner of his passions?

The answer came again to the forefront of her thoughts ... it all stemmed back to that Hallowe'en night, for he hadn't said: 'Dinah, let me make love to you?' He had taken ... taken until she felt there was nothing of herself left to give, only her sad and shaken heart and he hadn't asked for that.

Dinah knew that their sharing of each other tonight would turn to something else in the morning. Here in his big bed, in the darkness of their spent passion, all this meant was that her body which was to bear his child needed to be warmed, needed to be desired, needed to be appeased.

With a drowsy sigh Dinah closed her eyes and went off to sleep, dimly aware of a strong arm enclosing her.

When she awoke in the morning she was by herself in the kingsize bed. Birds were calling in the garden beyond the windows and, thank goodness, she felt not in the least sick and was longing for eggs and bacon, rolls and coffee and apricot jam.

She rolled to one side and pulled the service cord, and was reclining against Jason's pillow when Hester came into the room, looking trim and bright in her lace-collared dress.

'Jason told you I'd be in here, didn't he?'

'And about time too, if you don't mind me saying so, Miss Dinah!' Hester straightened the covers. 'I was brought up to believe in married folks sharing a bedroom.'

'Jason and I like our independence,' Dinah said airily.

'That's all very well in folks past the loving stage,' Hester rejoined. 'Are you feeling hungry? You look rosy enough, but I can always fetch you a biscuit and some water.'

'This morning I don't feel sick at all, isn't that strange?'

'Not strange at all, Miss Dinah. You slept with your man, didn't you?'

'Do you think that's the cure?' asked Dinah, with an air of innocence. 'Has Jason left for the bank?'

'I saw him making a telephone call. Do you want me to fetch him for you when he's finished talking?' Hester stood there regarding Dinah with a smile, for in the morning sunlight Dinah had the faintly flushed look to her skin that a cuddled child has; her hair was all fluffed up and she looked lost in the enormous bed.

'No, just be a dear and fetch me some breakfast.' Dinah ordered the menu which had been on her mind when she awoke. 'If Jason wants to speak to me, he'll come and see me of his own accord. Don't forget the jam, will you?'

'Are you eating in bed, Miss Dinah?'

'I might as well, as I'm the mistress of this great big establishment.' Dinah settled herself against the banked pillows. 'I must say this is a very comfortable bed. Trust Jason, nothing but the best for him!'

'He's a masterful man,' Hester said warmly, and went off to order Dinah's breakfast. When she returned with the laden tray Jason followed her into the room, looking tall, cool and collected in one of his well-cut business suits, a dense teakwood colour that fitted him like a second skin.

'Good morning, Dinah. Are you really going to eat all that food?'

'You try and stop me!' She looked up at him and he had such definition despite her hazy eyesight. 'You look like an advert for Brooks Brothers!'

'You, my dear, look like an advert for Peach Melba.' He sat down on the bed while Hester poured her coffee. 'I'm pleased you're in appetite—I've just been having a telephone chat with Dr Malcolm and she's advised me to tell Sothern that he's to cut down your posing time by half an hour.'

Dinah studied Jason over the rim of her coffee cup, and a faint look of fear shadowed her eyes. 'Why should she advise that?'

'Because neither she nor I want anything to go wrong with your pregnancy at three months. It's a perfectly reasonable request and nothing to get alarmed about.'

'Wouldn't you be alarmed?'

'I'm just being cautious—drink your coffee.'

'I'm the one who's in this condition, so I've a right to know if there's anything likely to go wrong,' Dinah insisted.

'Nothing is going wrong, we just don't want you overdoing the posing. Standing still can be very tiring.'

'It was your idea that I have my portrait painted. I—I sometimes wonder if you're expecting me to—die!'

'Don't be foolish.' He glanced at Hester. 'Be a good girl and leave us alone for a few minutes.'

Hester nodded, gave Dinah a slight frown and left the room. As the door closed quietly behind her, Jason leaned forward and captured Dinah's gaze with his determined eyes. 'I thought we'd exorcised a few of your fears, Dinah. Remember me? I'm the man who shared this bed with you last night, and now you're pushing me away again with your morbid talk about dying. As if I want you to die!'

'If that happened, Jason, you wouldn't have to tolerate the gossip when we get divorced. You know what people are like, they want their bankers to be upright, reliable citizens.'

'We'll discuss all that when the time comes,' he said curtly. 'In the meantime all you need to think about is having a healthy baby, and I'm mighty pleased that you fancy bacon and eggs first thing in the morning.'

'I—I think I've lost my appetite,' she said ungraciously. 'Hester can take the tray away——'

'Hester will do no such thing until that plate is cleared.' His gaze grew threatening. 'Don't think I'd hesitate to turn you over my knee if I thought a few spanks would cure you of this habit of opposing my wishes.'

'I'm sure you'd enjoy it,' she retorted.

'Calling me a bully?' Jason placed a hand on her bare shoulder inside the silky fold of her robe, stroking her skin with the tips of his fingers. 'Why do you have this impulse to spoil things between us, Dinah? Last night was ravishing, and not just for me, so admit it.'

'I—I'd had a nightmare,' she pulled away from his touch,' and I gave in to my schoolgirlish habit of running to you. You comforted me and I felt grateful.'

'Damn you, Dinah!' He stood up abruptly. 'You're turning into a little shrew, are you aware of it? That sweet side of you can't be trusted, and I'll give you fair warning, my girl. That's my child you're carrying and I don't want your neurosis to be inherited, so you'll smile when I say so. Eat when I give the order. And come to this damned bed whenever I click my fingers. Do you get the message?'

'Loud and clear.' She glared up at him. 'Now

I'm seeing the real Jason Devrel again—the one who loves giving orders and who takes his pleasure without a word of——' There she broke off and stuffed a piece of roll into her mouth.

'Word of *what*?' He leaned over her, insistently.

She chewed bread roll and obstinately refused to answer him. He straightened himself again. 'Very well, Dinah, we've laid a few things on the line, and you can take it from me that my signature is very much on that line. Understood?'

'Aye, aye, sir!' She gave him a mock salute. 'I'll be on parade whenever called, sir, and I'll obey you to the letter of the law. And when the time comes I'll make sure you do the same for me.'

'Meaning?' His brows were a menacing line above his dark eyes, and there was about him that look of the matador facing a raging bull.

'A certain document with your signature on it. It was stupid of me to argue about the settlement—I'm certainly earning every penny of it, and after my performance last night you should add a bonus!'

'You brat,' he said grittily. 'I had something to give you, but I don't think you deserve a present.'

'I'm not bothered about presents.' Dinah tucked into her bacon and eggs with sudden relish, having shown him that what had occurred between them last night had nothing to do with his winning ways or her sentimental feelings. It had been a mutually satisfying experience and that was all ... given time, and she had six months, and she'd become as armoured as he was.

He was on the point of leaving the room when he halted, thrust a hand into his pocket and took from it an oblong leather box. Without further comment he flung it down on the bed and strode from the room, leaving the door open so Hester could rejoin Dinah in the bedroom. Right away she noticed the jewel box and taking it from the foot of the bed handed it to Dinah.

'You open it,' Dinah said offhandedly. 'It's only payment for services rendered.'

'Miss Dinah!' Hester looked really shocked. 'I don't know how you can sit in that bed looking so innocent and talking in such a wicked way! Mr Jason is a gentleman, that's what he is! He's so pleased about that baby you're giving him that he feels like giving you things in return. You should be ashamed.'

'I should?' Dinah exclaimed. 'Jason Devrel's no saint, take it from me! He's a self-willed, arrogant so-and-so—oh, go on then, open the silly box! I know you're longing to see what's inside.'

'No, you should open it, Miss Dinah.' And Hester held out the box until Dinah grudgingly took it, springing the clasp to expose on black velvet a chain of pearl-blue opals.

Hester caught her breath in admiration. 'See how lucky you are, Miss Dinah. Aren't they the prettiest colour!'

Dinah lifted the opals from their bed, feeling a stab of contrition at the way she had spoken. 'Yes, they are nice,' she murmured.

'You should put them on right away, Miss Dinah,' Hester urged. 'Opals like to be next to a warm skin.'

'Do you suppose that's why Jason has given them to me?' Then Dinah gave a laugh at the look of reproof on Hester's face. 'Well, don't men like to be next to a warm skin?'

'Of course,' Hester agreed, 'but I think Mr Jason's just being kind and you should give him credit when it's due.'

'And what would you suggest is his due, Hester?'

'Well, I think,' Hester hesitated and blushed slightly, 'I think you ought to give him a kiss for each opal on that chain.'

'A very romantic notion,' Dinah scoffed, 'and straight out of a mushy love story!'

'I can't see anything wrong with love, Miss Dinah.' Hester lifted the tray from the bed and looked a trifle affronted. 'When I went in to tidy the bathroom I found your new dress all rolled up in the linen basket. Is it to be cleaned, miss?'

'No, my husband doesn't like it. It's to be taken down to the furnace and burned.'

'But it's new——'

'New and expensive, Hester, but it's to be burned to ashes.'

'It looked ever so nice on you——'

'Jason hates it, and his word is law in this house.' Dinah shrugged her shoulders. 'It caused a bad quarrel between us and I—I want to be rid of it.'

Looking mystified, Hester carried the tray to

the door. Dinah replaced the opals in their box and slid from Jason's bed, where last night she had been welcomed into his arms.

Tiny nerves quivered inside her like little bowstrings being drawn back and forth. 'You'll come to my bed whenever I click my fingers,' he had said this morning, and with a sigh she sought her slippers and walked out of his bedroom.

Had she vainly hoped that he might say something else to her?

CHAPTER NINE

DINAH made her way down the staircase in the violet riding habit, over her wrist the little loop which held up the skirt and stopped it from dragging. There was a great deal of material in the skirt and she certainly didn't want to trip over it, her mind shying away from an image of herself sprawled down there upon the solid oak floor.

Barry Sothern awaited her, rugged and big in a floppy white shirt and tan-coloured trousers. Like most artists he dressed casually, and it suited him.

The sun had died away and rain was beating against the big windows, so Barry had a photographer's lamp shining on to his easel. 'Shame the rain has set in,' he said. 'It pelted down last night, did you hear it?'

Dinah shook her head and felt a flow of warmth over her body, for last night she had been conscious of nothing except the rhythm of her pulses in response to Jason.

She took up her pose on the stairs, glad she could lean slightly against the baluster, for her legs felt trembly in the residue of emotion spent in Jason's arms.

Barry went to his easel and took up his brush. 'All ready?' he asked. 'I'm going to have to work a little faster from today; your lord and master has decreed that I cut down our time to an hour and a half. He certainly coddles you, Dinah.'

'It's the baby he's thinking about,' she rejoined. 'How am I shaping up on canvas—will I look a dignified wife and mother?'

'As a matter of fact,' said Barry, 'the background to your portrait is that wonderful stained glass window, and it's bringing out something almost gothic in your pose. You could be Jane Seymour shyly waiting for Tudor Hal to call upon you. How old is this house of Jason's?'

'Centuries old.' Dinah smiled at Barry's flight of fancy but wasn't displeased by it. In her wanderings around the house she had felt a strange affinity with its past history; its Jacobean style, its oak and carved stone, its mullioned windows and multi-chimneys had never oppressed her. It almost seemed like a stroke of destiny that she should be standing at the foot of the grand staircase, being portrayed on canvas so she could join those other women who had lived within these granite walls and loved or hated the Devrel master.

'The house has a ghost, did you know, Barry?' she said,

'Yes, I heard it mentioned in the village inn. The Devrels are of abiding interest to the locals, it would seem; they're already speculating on whether you're going to have a son or a daughter.'

'It's inevitable.' Her smile wavered, for it had to be common knowledge by now that Jason had married her for the baby's sake. 'Jason is the squire and he owns a great deal of Havenshore by inheritance. The Devrels have been fortunate in that their banking business has enabled them to support the land and the tenant farmers.'

'The villagers certainly speak well of their squire,' he agreed.

'He's good to them. No one can accuse Jason of not being a generous man, not only with his money but with time to spare for any troubles they might have.'

'Then why aren't you happy with him, Dinah?'

Barry's question seemed to go through her like a dart, for she knew what he meant by happiness. It was something unrelated to the pleasure which she had felt in Jason's embrace . . . it was elusive, and the yearning for it came in the reflective stillness that followed the rapture of the senses.

It was an emptiness of heart, where the beating was so loud when she sat through the evenings with Jason, when she listened to his music and then said goodnight and went her way to her bedroom.

'What doesn't he give you, this generous and thoughtful man?' Barry wanted to know.

She strove not to know the answer, but it was emblazoned across her mind and embedded in her heart. *His love.* From that very first day when she had walked into this house and seen the tall, tall figure standing beneath the stained glass window, strangely lit as the sun declined and the flame-gold rays shone down into the hall.

That tall figure had approached her and she had stood mesmerised by his dark eyes, only a little girl and certain he was the fire-robed angel Apollyon.

'Dinah, hold that faraway look, and do believe that I understand as a man but I have to be ruthless as an artist.'

'I was thinking,' she said, 'of the day I first came here and met Jason for the first time. I wonder if he knew how forbidding he looked to me?'

'Jason is a very deep and perceptive man, Dinah, so he had to realise his effect on you.'

'He towered over me and I—I wanted to dash out of the front door and hide from him. And as if he guessed, he lifted me up in his arms and carried me into his music room where the fire was leaping up the chimney and where hot muffins were waiting in a silver warmer.'

She gave a little sigh as the memories slid through her mind. 'Jason played his piano while I got butter all over my face, not to mention tears. What a funny little object I must have seemed to Jason! How strange it must have been for him to suddenly have a schoolgirl on his hands. Already people were thinking of him as a confirmed bachelor——'

She broke off as the telephone rang in the hall, with that imperative tone of demand that breaks into conversations and sets the pulses hammering.

'I'll answer it,' said Barry, 'you take a rest.'

Dinah slid down on to one of the stair treads as he strode across to the instrument and picked it up. He gave the Devrel number, then listened intently to the speaker on the other end of the line. Dinah watched him replace the receiver, then he turned towards her and thrust a hand through his mane of hair. It wasn't until he drew near to her that she could fully see that his expression was grim and worried.

'What's wrong?' She stood up and faced him. 'Was it Jason?'

Barry hesitated and they stood facing each other in the dim medley of colours that played upon them from the stained glass window. 'What's wrong?' Dinah demanded, and there was a rising note of alarm in her voice as she repeated the words, certain from the look on his face that whoever had telephoned had imparted some bad news.

'Dinah, perhaps you should sit down——'

'No,' her face whitened, 'just tell me a-and get it over with!'

'There's been some trouble down at the bank——'

'Jason's in trouble?' She clutched Barry's arm, unaware of stabbing her fingernails into him. 'I have to know!'

'Dinah, don't get yourself in a state!' He tried to propel her to one of the high-backed chairs that stood against the panelled wall.

'Don't do that,' she fought free of him, 'just tell me what that phone call was all about!'

'There's been an attempted robbery at the bank and several people have been hurt.'

'And Jason's one of them?'

'Dinah, you should sit down and try to be calm about this——'

'Calm?' she cried out, her face so white that her eyes looked almost frightening in their intensity. 'I can't sit here being calm—I have to go to him!'

Barry tried to restrain her. 'My dear girl, there isn't anything you can do——'

'What do you mean?' she broke in wildly. 'Is Jason killed——?'

'I doubt it, Dinah. The police are handling the situation and we must wait for further news.'

'It's Jason's bank and if anyone tried to rob him, he'd be furious and put up a fight!' Even as she spoke Dinah was hastening to the front door, impatient in the hampering skirt, half stumbling as she flung the door open and ran out on to the steps, hardly realising that she couldn't see them clearly. She was driven by a need so desperate it was without logic, and even as Barry cried out to her to be careful of the steps, the long skirt tripped her and she went hurtling downwards, screaming for Jason as she struck the stony treads one after another.

She finally lay still, a whimper of pain and shock all the sound she could make as Barry knelt beside her and gently fingered her neck, ensuring that she hadn't broken it.

Then as he gathered her up in his arms, her breath came back. 'My baby,' she sobbed. 'I've hurt my baby——'

'Hush, my dear.' Barry carried her up the steps and into the house, his voice raised to a bellow as he shouted for someone to come and help.

Dinah's head was slumped against his chest as she lost awareness of time and place . . . pain shot upwards through her body, and then everything dimmed and she didn't know anything more. She lay there unconscious in Barry's arms, the violet colour of the riding habit intensifying her pallor.

The tears that are sometimes wept during a sad dream were seeping down her face when Dinah stirred out of a long tranquillised sleep. 'Poor baby,' she whispered to herself. 'Poor Jason . . .'

A hand gripped hers and lips touched her wet cheek. 'Hello, little one,' a voice spoke out of the shadows that filled her head as she tried to come awake.

So that was it, she thought drowsily; she was dead and Jason was with her in that other life where people didn't have bodies that could be hurt and hearts that could break.

'It's the injection.' It was a different voice, from another direction. 'She's adrift in a kind of dream at present, unaware of any suffering.'

But I am suffering, Dinah tried to say. She knew it was all over, that life with Jason, so strange and troubled for both of them.

'She has tears on her face—Dinah's crying,' again that voice, penetrating the mist that whirled through her mind, where she wandered through the dreamland, half aware and half lost. 'Dinah, come back now—come back!'

She struggled to open her eyes, but the lids of her eyes were weighted and her lashes clung tearfully together. A dark shape leaned over her and warm, living lips laid kisses on her eyes, persisting until her eyes fluttered and opened and saw the lean and familiar face of a man who wasn't dead.

'Jason——?'

'I'm here beside you, Dinah.'

Her hazy eyes searched his face, finding beside her bed the one person in all the world who was always there when needed.

'Oh, Jason, my baby was killed!'

'No.' He cradled her face in his hands. 'Our baby is quite safe, snuggled cosy and warm where he belongs.'

'But I fell—I fell all the way down the front steps.' Her eyes were fixed upon Jason's face in the lamplight, searching for the real truth . . . he was afraid to tell her that the baby was lost.

'Listen to me, Dinah,' with his thumbs he wiped the tears from her cheeks, 'the bulk of the riding habit saved you from a bad fall which might have damaged the child.'

'But I—I feel pain——'

'You have a broken ankle, that's all.'

'Really—truthfully, Jason?' Hope began to tug at her heart, a little thread of joy tingled through her body.

'Would I lie to you, Dinah?'

'Yes!'

'In this instance, my dear, I'm not lying. Ask Dr Malcolm.'

The doctor leaned over Dinah from the other side of the bed and there was a reassuring smile on her face. 'You're carrying a tough young Devrel who's determined to stay in his cosy lodging until the time comes for him to emerge.

Your ankle will hurt a little, but you can bear it, can't you? I can't put you into plaster until the bone can be X-rayed at the hospital, and that should be in a day or two. All right?'

Dinah nodded, then looked again at Jason, as if in need of reassurance that he was really there . . . it was then she noticed the well-padded bandage around his upper left arm. 'Jason, you're hurt!'

'Only a bullet graze; nothing at all to worry yourself about.'

'I knew you were hurt!' She reached out and gently touched his arm. 'I knew you wouldn't let the bank be robbed—you waded in, didn't you?'

'There was a scrimmage.' His smile bordered on the grim. 'Damned pair of tykes, they winged a couple of our customers and I got my arm singed as I did a low-flying tackle from my rugger days. Anyway, the police arrived in record time, thanks to my assistant manager, who stamped on the alarm and got pistol-swiped, poor chap. He's in hospital with concussion, and if I had my way I'd strap those two layabouts in the old ducking cradle down in the village and duck them until they begged for mercy!'

Dinah didn't move her eyes from his face all the time he spoke, and neither of them heard Dr Malcolm quietly leave the room. They were alone, with the lamp making a pool of gold around them.

'Barry told me how you came to fall down the steps,' Jason said softly, and there in his eyes was the strangest look . . . Dinah wanted to search his eyes and learn what that look was all about, but the warmth of the bed, the relief of knowing that she hadn't lost the baby, these combined to make her drowsy. Her eyes began to close and as she fell asleep she was aware of Jason watching her ... always her guardian, there to see her safe through the perils of the night.

Sleep was a deep pool through which she floated ... soon she would ask, and perhaps he would tell her the secret of Hallowe'en night and unclose that door which had always stood closed between them. This time she smiled in her sleep instead of weeping.

Dinah lay there in the solarium, listening lazily to the seabirds. They flew joyously over the waves and now and again one would flash down into the water and scoop up a fish. Today the sky was a pale blue with a fluff of cloud, and beyond the glass walls of the sun room lay a scene that Turner might have painted ... a seascape full of dancing light and changing shades of blue and grey as the sea rolled in against the cliffs.

She watched contentedly, a hand against that swell of her body where that small heart ticked quietly in the baby she now loved with such a fierce protectiveness ... so little and helpless and so much a part of her; so wanted that it hurt.

Though she was unsure of Jason's intention with regard to their life together, one thing was certain, the baby was hers as much as his, and even if they were never meant to live as her heart yearned, as lovers bound by their heart-strings, she would stay and see her child grow up to enjoy the many delights of this high old house on Devrel Drive, with its towers of stone and its gabled wings stretched across the wide courtyard.

Wings seemed to flutter inside her when she caught the sound of footfalls, firm and familiar. Jason entered the solarium, tall in sweater and breeches, kneeboots clasping his long legs. She knew he had been out riding, for she had seen him galloping Moonlight along the far down beach, racing the black horse into the spume, so vigorous and alive.

'You look at ease.' He smiled as he crossed the solarium towards her. 'Is the ankle feeling more comfortable now you have it plastered?'

She nodded, a strange shyness gripping her by the throat when he leaned down to brush a kiss across her cheek. 'You have a little more colour, Dinah, and the bruise is fading from your brow.'

'I feel heaps better,' she assured him. 'I was watching you down on the beach taking a canter on Moonlight and I—I so longed to join you.'

'The ankle won't take too long to mend.' He sat down on the foot of the lounger, and though the weren't touching Dinah felt him in her very bones.

'By the time my ankle's mended,' she said, 'I shall be too big to ride, and I wouldn't want to take the risk.'

'No,' his chin was set and firm, 'I don't want you taking any more risks, and I'm cursing myself for suggesting that you wear that riding habit; it was obviously the cause of your fall.'

She couldn't suppress a shiver at the way she

had hurtled down the steps, quite certain in her mind that her child would be hurt or lost when she hit the ground. But when she had gone to the hospital to have her ankle attended to, Dr Malcolm had carried out further tests to ensure that all was well with her pregnancy. Even though the riding skirt had tripped her, its yards of material had also cushioned her where it mattered and the baby was quite safe, the heartbeat steady and regular.

Unlike Dinah's, for the dark and powerful figure of Jason on the end of the lounger was doing chaotic things to her heart; when his eyes brushed her face her breath seemed to quicken: when she looked into his dark eyes she saw again that half-pained, almost uncertain look ... and never had she seen Jason look uncertain about anything.

'It was such a relief about the baby, wasn't it?' she said breathlessly. 'I'd have died if any-thing——'

'I wouldn't have let you die,' he said fiercely. 'What would I have left if I——'

He broke off in mid-sentence, and Dinah was crying out silently for him to say it would hurt ... hurt like hell if he lost her. Now she could feel herself holding her breath, her hand reaching to be possessed as he leaned nearer to her.

'I see you're wearing the opals,' he murmured. 'I'm glad.'

'They're very pretty, Jason.'

'They remind me of your eyes.'

'Oh,' she flushed as if she were still a schoolgirl

whom he could confuse with his worldly aloofness and culture, 'my silly eyes that can't see for looking.'

'Look well at me, Dinah, for I have something to say and I'm finding it difficult.' Slowly his fingers squeezed hers until she could feel her wedding band pressing into her flesh and bone. 'When I sat at your bedside, my dear, after you took that painful fall, I knew that never again would I force my hand where you're concerned. What I'm trying to say is this—if you would like to go away and be apart from me in the coming months, then I shall abide by your wish and arrange all the details. Perhaps a country cottage would be nice, or maybe you'd prefer to stay at some quiet hotel——?'

'I couldn't bear to stay at some horrible hotel!'

'Then a cottage——?'

'No!'

'Tell me what you want, Dinah, I know you're set on being an independent working girl, but it will be some time before you can go back to your figurines and that bossy supervisor who looked as if she ate china plates for breakfast.'

'Are you trying to get rid of me?' Dinah asked, trying to get free of the hand that suddenly reached for her and was pulling her into an embrace of such force and passion that she was rendered quite helpless.

'Does it feel as if I am?' He gazed down at her with the look of naked passion he had revealed on Hallowe'en night. 'You don't know—can't know what a personal hell I've been through, wanting you not as a girl I was supposed to guard but as someone who felt like part of me. From that first day, Dinah, you were as much a part of this house as I was. For years it had felt so empty, and then came the day when you walked in, and never—never was I going to permit you to walk out again!'

He broke off and buried his face in her warm throat, and Dinah lay there, closely gathered to him, and like a person in a dream all movement and speech was barred to her by the dictates of the dream. She couldn't move a hand, she couldn't say a word, she could only listen at last to his confession.

'I told myself you needed a father and I tried to be a parent to you.' His lips moved against her skin, making the words even more intimate. 'For those first years I succeeded and I hoped that you thought of me as a deputy parent, but then you started to turn into a young woman and I could feel myself wanting you not as my ward but as someone far closer in every way. When I attended your graduation and I watched you go to the podium for your diploma, you looked so sweet, so vulnerable in contrast to some of those other girls with their assured manner, their certainty of themselves.'

Jason paused and kissed her mouth with a hunger of tenderness that shook her to the heart. 'You were different, my Dinah. You had a sensitivity that seemed to shine through your skin. I could see it, but I knew that out there in that brash and demanding world you would be